FRANCIS \
DEAD OPPOSITE

Francis Vivian was born Arthur Ernest Ashley in 1906 at East Retford, Nottinghamshire. He was the younger brother of noted photographer Hallam Ashley. Vivian laboured for a decade as a painter and decorator before becoming an author of popular fiction in 1932. In 1940 he married schoolteacher Dorothy Wallwork, and the couple had a daughter.

After the Second World War he became assistant editor at the Nottinghamshire Free Press and circuit lecturer on many subjects, ranging from crime to bee-keeping (the latter forming a major theme in the Inspector Knollis mystery *The Singing Masons*). A founding member of the Nottingham Writers' Club, Vivian once awarded first prize in a writing competition to a young Alan Sillitoe, the future bestselling author.

The Dean Street Press mysteries were published between 1941 and 1959. In the novels, ingenious plotting and fair play are paramount. A colleague recalled that 'the reader could always arrive at a correct solution from the given data. Inspector Knollis never picked up an undisclosed clue which, it was later revealed, held the solution to the mystery all along.'

Francis Vivian died on April 2, 1979 at the age of 73.

FRANCIS VIVIAN MYSTERIES
Available from Dean Street Press

FRANCIS VIVIAN

DEAD OPPOSITE THE CHURCH

With an introduction by Curtis Evans

DEAN STREET PRESS

INTRODUCTION

SHORTLY BEFORE his death in 1951, American agriculturalist and scholar Everett Franklin Phillips, then Professor Emeritus of Apiculture (beekeeping) at Cornell University, wrote British newspaperman Arthur Ernest Ashley (1906-1979), author of detective novels under the pseudonym Francis Vivian, requesting a copy of his beekeeping mystery *The Singing Masons*, the sixth Inspector Gordon Knollis investigation, which had been published the previous year in the United Kingdom. The eminent professor wanted the book for Cornell's Everett F. Phillips Beekeeping Collection, "one of the largest and most complete apiculture libraries in the world" (currently in the process of digitization at Cornell's The Hive and the Honeybee website). Sixteen years later Ernest Ashely, or Francis Vivian as I shall henceforward name him, to an American fan requesting an autograph ("Why anyone in the United States, where I am not known," he self-deprecatingly observed, "should want my autograph I cannot imagine, but I am flattered by your request and return your card, duly signed.") declared that fulfilling Professor Phillip's donation request was his "greatest satisfaction as a writer." With ghoulish relish he added, "I believe there was some objection by the Librarian, but the good doctor insisted, and so in it went! It was probably destroyed after Dr. Phillips died. Stung to death."

After investigation I have found no indication that the August 1951 death of Professor Phillips, who was 73 years old at the time, was due to anything other than natural causes. One assumes that what would have been the painfully ironic demise of the American nation's most distinguished apiculturist from bee stings would have merited some mention in his death notices. Yet Francis Vivian's fabulistic claim otherwise provides us with a glimpse of that mordant sense of humor and storytelling relish which glint throughout the eighteen mystery novels Vivian published between 1937 and 1959.

Ten of these mysteries were tales of the ingenious sleuthing exploits of series detective Inspector Gordon Knollis, head of the Burnham C.I.D. in the first novel in the series and a Scotland Yard detective in the rest. (Knollis returns to Burnham in later novels.) The debut Inspector Knollis mystery, *The Death of Mr. Lomas*, which was published in 1941, is actually the seventh Francis Vivian detective novel. However, after the Second World War, when the author belatedly returned to his vocation of mystery writing, all of the remaining detective novels he published, with two exceptions, chronicle the criminal cases of the keen and clever Knollis. These other Inspector Knollis tales are: *Sable Messenger* (1947), *The Threefold Cord* (1947), *The Ninth Enemy* (1948), *The Laughing Dog* (1949), *The Singing Masons* (1950), *The Elusive Bowman* (1951), *The Sleeping Island* (1951), *The Ladies of Locksley* (1953) and *Darkling Death* (1956). (Inspector Knollis also is passingly mentioned in Francis Vivian's final mystery, published in 1959, *Dead Opposite the Church*.) By the late Forties and early Fifties, when Hodder & Stoughton, one of England's most important purveyors crime and mystery fiction, was publishing the Francis Vivian novels, the Inspector Knollis mysteries had achieved wide popularity in the UK, where "according to the booksellers and librarians," the author's newspaper colleague John Hall later recalled in the Guardian (possibly with some exaggeration), "Francis Vivian was neck and neck with Ngaio Marsh in second place after Agatha Christie." (Hardcover sales and penny library rentals must be meant here, as with one exception--a paperback original--Francis Vivian, in great contrast with Crime Queens Marsh and Christie, both mainstays of Penguin Books in the UK, was never published in softcover.)

John Hall asserted that in Francis Vivian's native coal and iron county of Nottinghamshire, where Vivian from the 1940s through the 1960s was an assistant editor and "colour man" (writer of local color stories) on the Nottingham, or Notts, *Free Press*, the detective novelist "through a large stretch of the coalfield is reckoned the best local author after Byron and D. H. Lawrence." Hall added that "People who wouldn't know Alan Sillitoe from George Eliot will stop Ernest in the street and tell him they solved his last detective story." Somewhat ironically, given this assertion, Vivian in his capacity as a founding member of the Nottingham Writers Club awarded first prize in a 1950 Nottingham writing competition to no other than 22-year-old local aspirant Alan Sillitoe, future "angry young man" author of *Saturday Night and Sunday Morning* (1958) and *The Loneliness of the Long Distance Runner* (1959). In his 1995 autobiography Sillitoe recollected that Vivian, "a crime novelist who earned his living by writing . . . gave [my story] first prize, telling me it was so well written and original that nothing further need be done, and that I should try to get it published." This was "The General's Dilemma," which Sillitoe later expanded into his second novel, *The General* (1960).

While never himself an angry young man (he was, rather, a "ragged-trousered" philosopher), Francis Vivian came from fairly humble origins in life and well knew how to wield both the hammer and the pen. Born on March 23, 1906, Vivian was one of two children of Arthur Ernest Ashley, Sr., a photographer and picture framer in East Retford, Nottinghamshire, and Elizabeth Hallam. His elder brother, Hallam Ashley (1900-1987), moved to Norwich and became a freelance photographer. Today he is known for his photographs, taken from the 1940s through the 1960s, chronicling rural labor in East Anglia (many of which were collected in the 2010 book *Traditional Crafts and Industries in East Anglia:*

The Photographs of Hallam Ashley). For his part, Francis Vivian started working at age 15 as a gas meter emptier, then labored for 11 years as a housepainter and decorator before successfully establishing himself in 1932 as a writer of short fiction for newspapers and general magazines. In 1937, he published his first detective novel, *Death at the Salutation.* Three years later, he wed schoolteacher Dorothy Wallwork, with whom he had one daughter.

After the Second World War Francis Vivian's work with the Notts *Free Press* consumed much of his time, yet he was still able for the next half-dozen years to publish annually a detective novel (or two), as well as to give popular lectures on a plethora of intriguing subjects, including, naturally enough, crime, but also fiction writing (he published two guidebooks on that subject), psychic forces (he believed himself to be psychic), black magic, Greek civilization, drama, psychology and beekeeping. The latter occupation he himself took up as a hobby, following in the path of Sherlock Holmes. Vivian's fascination with such esoterica invariably found its way into his detective novels, much to the delight of his loyal readership.

As a detective novelist, John Hall recalled, Francis Vivian "took great pride in the fact that the reader could always arrive at a correct solution from the given data. His Inspector never picked up an undisclosed clue which, it was later revealed, held the solution to the mystery all along." Vivian died on April 2, 1979, at the respectable if not quite venerable age of 73, just like Professor Everett Franklin Phillips. To my knowledge the late mystery writer had not been stung to death by bees.

Curtis Evans

My dear Cecil:

It is twenty-one years since I walked into your office and asked you to review my first novel, please, dear kind sir. Except that you said it humorously, you then told me more or less what Packman tells Charlie Carrington in this story. So when, years later, you suggested that I should write a yarn round a weekly newspaper office, I firstly decided to get to know my subject—as I did with beekeeping and archery—before writing about it, and secondly to use the opening you had unwittingly provided. I think you will appreciate it.

Neither of us realised at the time that I should eventually enter the profession of journalism, nor that for a short time I should be saddled with the editorship of a weekly newspaper. Even if the directors only dubbed me Temporary (Very) Acting Editor, I still had the work to do, and with a very small staff, so that but for the help of yourself and our works' overseer I should have been up the creek. It was very much to your professional disadvantage to help my rival paper, but with your never-failing greatness of heart you did so. Such things are not easily forgotten, and so here is your story. *En passant*, one day I'll write you one about a village pageant!

The story is written round the old building in which died, in its 98th year, the newspaper whose slogan I have used as my title. Why and how it died is another story which probably only Brooky can tell, but the staff is scattered over the country, and the old flatbed sold for scrap. The characters are necessarily invented, for what reader could possibly believe in the ones that worked on the old Twelve-Page Miracle? In the interests of the lay readers I have reduced some technical and craft terms to plain English.

And so I offer my thanks to you, Brooky, Jack, and David, editors one and all. Without your help I should have missed a great deal of fun, more trouble than any one man should be expected to endure, and the pleasure of writing the first and last dedicatory epistle to appear in any novel by,

Yours sincerely,

FRANCIS VIVIAN.

1
FORTY-EIGHT-POINT CENTURY

THE BEGINNING of life and the end of death are mysteries that have intrigued thinking men since the earliest moments of recorded time. The end of life, and the beginning of death, are equally baffling enigmas that seem insoluble. At what point, for instance, in the life of Edward John Packman, owner-editor of the *Borough News*, did the Angel of Death put his finger on him and say "You are mine!"

Johnny Crompton, the slim and fair-haired chief reporter of the Carrbank weekly paper, said that Edward John knocked the first nail into his coffin four and a half years before Danny Moss murdered his sweetheart, and when Danny made his first appearance in Juvenile Court.

Charlie Carrington, the town's local author, who sometimes freelanced for Edward John, said the whole business began eighteen years before, at the instant when Packman senior died of cerebral thrombosis, and Edward John became part-owner and editor-manager.

"Edward John had just stepped into his father's shoes when I first met him," said Carrington, a lean and silver-thatched man of forty-five. "He was quite a character even then. Let me tell you how I met him that Wednesday morning eighteen years ago . . ."

As Carrington was shown into his office, Packman was playing The Editor, busily checking page proofs, and initialling them with a great deal of consequence and flourish. Even then he wore the chalk-striped blue suits and multi-coloured bows that were characteristic features throughout his life, and he smoked a steady forty cigarettes a day through an Edgar-Wallace holder.

In due course he deigned to look up. "Well?" he said brusquely.

"My name is Charles Carrington. I've written a book," Carrington informed him diffidently.

"God help you!" said Packman.

He had not at that time achieved the fat sleekness of later years, and the smile that creased his thin face was little more than a sneer. "So what?"

"My publisher's sent you a review copy."

Packman nodded heavily.

"And you are going to ask if I can spare you space for a review—which you'll expect to be good and also long. You'll call it publicity, but it's really advertising for which you won't have to pay, and it will put pounds into your pocket at the expense of the *Borough News*."

He paused to let that sink in, and then asked: "What's the thing called?"

The review copy was lying at the back of his desk, its jacket a minor work of art. The title was limned across a colourful inn signboard, and the background was a symbolical stormy sky.

"That's the one," said Carrington.

Packman's manner eased somewhat. He gave Carrington what was nearly a friendly smile.

"So you wrote it, eh? Not at all bad for a first novel. I finished it in bed last night. Yes, I have to admit that you show promise, Mr. er—er?"

"Carrington."

"And you live in Carrbank?"

Packman reached for a wad of copy paper. "We'd better have a few biographical notes. I think we might manage to spare you a stick or so of space. I can take a photo as well if you have one."

It was only in later years that Carrington realised his entry that morning was a God-sent one to Packman, who was wondering what the heck to fill with this week.

Anyway, Packman thawed even more when he learned that Carrington was a journalist, albeit a freelance, and had kept himself alive by writing for ten years before attempting this first novel.

He reached for the book, looked at the jacket appraisingly, and smiled.

"We get so many people trying to write, people who have never even smelled printers' ink. How the devil can they expect to write without training? Writing's a trade and it has to be learned—the hard way. You know that!"

With a full memory of kipper and porridge diets in the early days of his career, Carrington was well able to nod his agreement.

"They think they can buy a fountain pen and a ream of quarto bond, and go right ahead into the big money," Packman continued. "And yet, I ask you, would either of us be mug enough to buy a slab of marble and expect to hack a masterpiece from it like—hm, what's the man's name?"

By now Carrington reckoned he had Edward John weighed up, and so he replied: "Einstein."

"That's him," said Packman. "Anyway, in some respects you are one of us, and you've obviously been through the mill, and so we'll help you. I'll do the review myself."

Carrington thanked him.

Packman leaned back in the editorial chair and prodded invisible points in the air with his 2B subbing pencil.

"You know the rules, Mr. Carrington. You've written a novel—a good novel, let me say. From now on you're news. It don't matter a damn to me whether you commit bigamy, get divorced, steal half a quid and get caught, get a Birthday Honour, an honorary degree, or get chopped to pieces under a train. You are our new Local Author with initial caps, and *news* hereafter. . . ."

He glanced at Carrington to see how he was taking it, and went on: "Never come crawling to me and ask to be kept out of my paper. My rule is *Even My Own Granny!* There can be no exceptions. Once you make an exception, then someone can come along and claim precedent."

He waved a magnificent hand.

"See me again about a fortnight before your next novel is to be published, and we'll do a preliminary par or two about you. And don't forget to send me a photo."

He showed Carrington down the stairs, through the general office, and to the street, where he slapped him on the back and wished him good fortune. Then he sent for the junior, gave him Carrington's novel, and said: "Take this bloody thing to Canon Bodley and ask him to do a column review. Tell him to take his finger out. I want it quick." That, of course, was something else Carrington did not know until later years when he more or less haunted the office.

He gave Carrington a good review, and thereafter Carrington prospered, more due to his own efforts than to those of Edward John.

A lot happened in the next eighteen years. After the death of Packman senior the throne was shared by Edward John and his sister Amelia. Amelia was younger than Edward John, and she married Tommy Grosvenor, founder of the town's now-famous radio-manufacturing firm. This was about the time that Carrington was slaving on his first novel. Their daughter, Lisbeth Ann, was born a fortnight after the book was reviewed.

The gestation periods of books and babies are similar, but whereas Carrington made mistakes and had to correct them, Amelia made no mistakes at all and produced a lovely piece of work.

Tommy Grosvenor travelled the world selling his goods, and took to private flying as a means of speeding up business and saving time. In due course Lisbeth Ann went to a private school on the south coast, and Tommy began taking Amelia with him on overseas trips. Then there was an accident, and both were killed in Kenya while Tommy was trying to come in to land crosswind on a narrow strip. The world lost a modern merchant adventurer, and a gentle and beautiful lady. Lisbeth Ann became part-owner presumptive of the paper, and the estates of her father and mother were held in trust until she was twenty-one.

Throughout these eighteen years Edward John had remained unmarried to everything but the paper, although he enjoyed a few extra-marital adventures on the side. At home he was capably looked after by old Mrs. Barrowcliffe, who had been his nanny, and who still looked on him as a newborn, probably because his scalp was as bare of covering as his other end had been when she first powdered it. He took Lisbeth Ann into his home, and found her a job as junior reporter on the paper so that she would know something about journalism by the time she joined him as an equal financial partner.

Johnny Crompton had joined the paper as chief reporter two years before the murder, and as soon as Lisbeth Ann's eyes settled on him she fell in love with him. He was everything she had ever hoped for, all rolled into one. Johnny saw her as a nice girl, rosy-cheeked and dark-eyed. She favoured swirling circular skirts and gay colours, and her appearance was flattered rather than spoiled by a modern haircut which looked as if a horse had nibbled round the edges, and then obligingly licked up the ragged ends with its tongue.

She had a reliable shorthand note of ninety words a minute, could write good straightforward Anglo-Saxon, and was friendly and conscientious. So to Johnny she was a junior reporter, a colleague:

> *A primrose by the river's brim,*
> *A dicotyledon was to him;*
> *And it was nothing more.*

The other members of the *News* staff were Harry Davidson, who did most of the inquests and borough court work, and young Bill Seymour, also a junior, who devoted his time to local sport.

Eighteen years of editorship had not improved Edward John Packman in any way. He had reached the age of fifty-six, and was now tubby, dogmatic, and at times as cantankerous as a bear with a sore head, particularly on Thursday nights, when he put the paper to bed ready for its early rising next morning.

He had persisted in his "Even your own granny" policy, and it had become a religion with him—he practised no other, anyway. He did not care a damn whom he upset or offended, and he had smacked down on so many burgesses of Carrbank that the paper had become known as *Packman's Pillory*.

It did not matter whether you landed yourself in court for some minor offence or outsize felony, or made an ass of yourself when delivering an after-dinner speech when the wine had flowed too well; you were in the pillory at the weekend. And heaven help any of his reporters who played down a story for any reason whatever!

Carrington, meanwhile, had continued to write two detection novels a year, with short stories in between as a form of financially profitable relaxation. He made good friends among the county police, and was grateful to them for the help they gave him in regard to procedure. From time to time he helped out with the reporting of quarter sessions and assizes, and it was this intrusion into real-life crime that brought about the only row he ever had with Edward John, and it was over Danny Moss.

It started slightly more than four and a half years before Packman's murder. Danny, then a schoolboy, landed in a minor scrape that took him into Juvenile Court at the behest of an over-zealous constable who should, instead, have swiped him over the ears with his gloves. Danny emerged after a lecture from the magistrate, and a fine of five shillings levied for trespassing on a railway embankment. Danny insisted that he was looking for wild strawberries, and the constable said he was acting suspiciously in the neighbourhood of a platelayers' hut.

Packman, by law, could not use the names of juveniles who appeared at the court, but he did everything else he could get away with in the interest of a good story—and his rooted objection to the suppression of news of any kind. By the time he had rewritten the reporter's story his readers were left in no doubt that "this young delinquent" was Danny Moss (15), of 34, Ludlow Court, Carrbank.

Danny responded to this publicity, and was also a hero to his pals, so six months later he made an appearance for shop-breaking. He pleaded that he stole nothing from the shop, and only wanted to prove to his pals that he was capable of breaking in. He was put on probation for two years, and broke it four months later when he forced the lock of a tobacco kiosk and stole cigarettes which he did not smoke.

From then on his story was one of evolution from bad to worse, and finally, when he was nineteen and a half, he strangled his sweetheart because she insisted on remaining a virgin. He raped her, strangled her, and then went to the police station and gave himself up.

Even a dog is not supposed to go into court with a bad name, but thanks to Packman's publicity over the years Danny was no unknown quantity when he first appeared before a special court at Carrbank, and later at the committal proceedings that forwarded him to Burnham Assizes.

It was a few days before committal that Packman sent for Carrington.

"It's this way, Charlie," he said. "Young Moss comes up on Tuesday, and it's certain he'll be sent up for trial. I want you to do the descriptive intros to both stories—committal and assize. Johnny will do the verbatim stuff. At the committal you are to turn on the sob-stuff and build up the emotional aspect—sobbing mother, despairing father, and the same for the parents of the murdered girl, with added touches of restrained anger as they gaze at Danny in the dock. Don't forget to drag in at least twice that she was only Sweet Seventeen, with caps. Readers really go for that stuff!

"For the assize I shall want more colour than anything else. Contrast the judge's scarlet robe with the traditional dark oak of the panelling and furniture. Bring in the wigs and gowns, and the odd splash of colour from the dress of some woman in the public seats, even if you have to invent it. Oh, and work in a moment of pregnant silence when nothing is heard but the scratch of a quill pen on parchment."

"Don't be a bloody fool," said Carrington. "They use typers and quarto these days."

"What the hell does that matter?" demanded Packman. "How many of my hundred thousand readers—five to a copy—will be in court, anyway? How many of the clots attend? They're as ignorant as sin, anyway, and will sooner believe that yarn than the truth. Two-fifty words of committal, and three hundred of assize. Leave the straight stuff entirely to Crompton."

Carrington shook his head slowly. "I've done some jobs for you in the past, E.J., and I'm grateful for all you've done for me, but this is one job I won't do."

"Like hell you will!" said Packman.

"Like hell I won't," said Carrington as he got up and moved to the door.

"And why not, might I ask?"

Carrington hesitated, and then told him a lie. "It isn't up my street."

"It's up your street to write crime stories, and to do glamourised versions of the real-life investigations of Burnell and those other Scotland Yard flatfoots. If you can do that you can write up a dirty little murderer like Danny Moss!"

"Sorry," said Carrington, and let himself out.

He did not wish to offend Packman further by telling him that, like nearly every other thinking person in the town, he believed that Danny would never have got so near to knocking on the door of the condemned cell but for Edward John's build-up of his misdemeanours as a lad.

Danny was committed for trial, and tried, and sentenced to death. There was an appeal, but according to the appeal judges there was not a single redeeming feature, the case was sound in law, there was no misdirection of the jury by the judge, and it was a most revolting crime for the basest of motives.

A petition of three thousand signatures, nearly all different, was organised, but the Home Secretary saw no reason to advise Her Majesty the Queen, and Danny was due to be hanged by Teddy Jessop at nine o'clock on the morning of September 18th, which was a Friday.

On the previous Wednesday the headline for the front page was sent down to the case-room to be set. It was in forty-eight-point Century type, to run clean across the top of the front page: YOUNG THUG'S CAREER ENDS. The *Borough News* was due to be on the streets at half-past seven in the morning, an hour and a half before Danny Moss was hanged. By nine o'clock on Thursday night, Edward John Packman was dead, and the hunt for his murderer was on.

2
THE DAY OF WRATH

THE REPORTERS' ROOM was heavy with yesterday's bad air as Johnny Crompton kicked open the door at nine o'clock the next morning. Mingled with the fug of the shag tobacco smoked by Davidson was the stale odour of the new perfume which Lisbeth Ann had discovered and was using too enthusiastically, and the minty flavour of the humbugs sucked by young Seymour as he tried to cut down his cigarette bill. Crompton stuck his own cigarette in the corner of his mouth and strode across the room to pull down the upper sashes of the two large windows that occupied nearly the whole of the southern wall, overlooked the main street, St. Gudulph's Gate, and stared straight into the northern windows of St. Gudulph's Church. He glanced at the three desks to make sure that all who had been working the previous evening had returned to write up their copy, and then went along the corridor to his own room.

A sheet of copy paper lay in the middle of his desk. He knew what was written on it without reading it, because such pieces of paper, placed so conspicuously first thing in the morning, always bore the same legend: *See me, E.J.P.* They usually meant trouble.

Crompton turned to the mirror propped against the wall over the mantelpiece, fumbled a comb from his outer breast pocket, and ran it through his thick fair hair. He paused in the process to regard himself critically. He was of medium height, fresh-complexioned, clean-shaven, and, he had to admit, looking more dissipated than he should at the age of twenty-seven. There were dark crescents under his eyes, and the whites had acquired a jaundiced tinge.

He grimaced at his reflection. He was a darned fool for letting the job get him down, and a bigger darned fool for going on the binge at the Golden Falcon. It was no way of forgetting Danny Moss. After all, what was one more hanged murderer? What did it matter if Danny was only a youth? He had murdered the girl when she was defending her honour, and he deserved to die—or did he?

The door behind him opened, and a caustic voice said:— "When you've finished admiring yourself, Crompton, I'd like to see you. I left a note on your desk."

"I saw, I read, I concurred," said Crompton, but the owner of the voice had gone, and the door was closed.

There came a rapid tip-tapping of light shoes on the stairs from the ground floor which continued along the corridor to the reporters' room, and then the door was slammed. Muffled sobbing reached him through the lath and plaster wall.

"Oh God—women!" Crompton exclaimed.

He flicked a falling quiff of hair from his forehead and went quietly to the reporters' room. Lisbeth Ann was slumped in her chair. Her arms were down on the desk and her face was hidden in them, and she was sobbing her heart out.

Crompton sat on the corner of the desk, and laid a hand on her shoulder. "What's the son of a bitch done this time?"

He lifted her head, and dabbed ineffectively at her eyes with his handkerchief. "You're a pretty girl, and you're going to spoil your looks, and then I'll have to send Seymour to the Tory Women's meeting at the Falcon this afternoon, and you'll miss a good free tea and a lot of useless natter."

She pushed him away, and pressed her handkerchief to her mouth. "You're—you're making fun of me!" she sniffed.

Crompton shook his head. "I wouldn't do that, Lisbeth Ann. It isn't a day for making fun. There'll be wild words, hell, and high water before we go to press tonight. In fact someone may get the push. Anyway, what's your trouble?"

"Uncle John . . ." she faltered.

"I guessed that," said Crompton, "but Uncle John doing what?"

"He—he kicked Omar Khayyam, and I've taken him to the vet, and he says Uncle John has ruptured his stomach and he'll have to destroy him—put him to sleep."

"Good idea at that," Crompton murmured to himself.

She broke into sobs again.

Crompton lit a cigarette, and waited until she was calmer.

"Now then," he asked, "who the heck is Omar Whatsit?"

"My—my Persian kitten. He was only playing with Uncle John's shoelace while he was having breakfast, and Uncle John lashed out with his foot and kicked him into the hearth. . . ."

"The louse," said Crompton.

"I wish Dad and Mum were alive!"

"Don't we all," said Crompton.

"I'll run away. . . ."

"To where?"

"I'll get a job in Fleet Street, and share a flat with someone."

"On the wages which this great profession pays its juniors you'd have to share it with a sugar daddy, or do part-time work on Curzon Street, my girl," said Crompton. "Don't talk damned silly!"

"Johnny, does my—my nose shine?"

"Like a good deed in a naughty world," quoted Crompton. "I'd hop off and powder it before the lads come in. I'll meanwhile go and have my own morning session with Edward John. If you hear shots, send for the police!"

"A row over Danny Moss?"

"A first-class row over Danny Moss!"

Lisbeth Ann did a couple of sniffs before she said: "You don't like the way Uncle John runs this paper, do you, Johnny?"

"Who could that possesses a conscience? So far as Danny is concerned, this newspaper sent him to the rope."

"But he did murder Stella Wellesley, Johnny!"

"Edward John strangled her," Crompton said savagely.

He broke off. "Sounds like Davy and Bill coming in. You'd better shoot to the toilet and get your war-paint on."

Lisbeth Ann laid a hand on his arm. "Johnny, you won't let Uncle John sack you, will you?"

"I'll resign first," grinned Crompton.

They left the reporters' room together, and passed Davidson and Seymour on the corridor. Davidson glanced at Lisbeth Ann, and raised an eyebrow to Crompton. "Trouble?" he asked.

"Double, double, toil and trouble," Crompton re-plied.

He strode on, tapped at Packman's door, and went in.

"I expected you twenty minutes ago," said Packman.

"The buses weren't running," replied Crompton.

"Yesterday afternoon," said Packman, "I asked you to write up the Danny Moss copy for the front page. Two double-column pars, and the rest in single. I haven't seen it yet."

"I haven't written it," said Crompton.

"Let me have it within the hour," said Packman. "Old Turner's got double col on his machine just now, and he'll be wanting to change by half-past ten. That's all."

Crompton opened his mouth, and closed it again. He left the office quietly.

Davidson and Seymour were waiting for him in his own room.

Davidson, long, lean and sardonic-lipped, asked: "What's brewing, Johnny? What's wrong with the bint?"

"Oh, the old boy kicked her kitten across the hearth this morning, bust its innards, and she's had to have it destroyed."

"We-ell, he always went for the defenceless, so what?" murmured Davidson. "And what's biting you? Danny Moss?"

Crompton leaned against the mantelpiece. "Look, Davy, we have a code of ethics in this profession. Are we supposed to observe them, or should we merely read 'em and then forget 'em?"

"The Greeks believed in moderation in all things—even in observing moderation," said Davidson. "All depends on the circs, old boy."

"Don't you think we've hammered Danny Moss enough, without going to town on Friday morning to hammer his parents?"

"If the lad had been brought up proper like what we are he wouldn't have gone wrong," Davidson said mockingly. He then went serious. "You weren't in court all the way through, Johnny. It was a rotten job, and if hanging is the punishment for such jobs, then he should hang. As a newspaper we represent the folk who weren't present in court, and it's our duty to tell them what we saw and heard."

He raised a warning finger as Crompton began to reply. "Just a minute, Johnny. I hadn't finished. It's our job to give hard news—but we should be fair, and we should keep out comment. That's what's biting you, isn't it? I've seen that forty-eight-point head down on the stone. It's pretty bloody, I agree, but at the same time we have to admit that we work for Packman, and if that's what Packman wants from us then that's what we have to supply. Packman can always argue that if you don't like the conditions you can leave. Must see both sides of it, old boy!"

Crompton shrugged, and went to his desk for the diary. "We'd better get on with the day's work. See, you've the Young Farmers' job, and the cage birds. I've the Carpenter inquest at eleven, and the rest of the day in here."

He turned to Seymour. "Get your sports topics out of the way as soon as you can, and don't forget you've a play to do tonight. Lisbeth Ann has the Tory Women's annual natter

this afternoon, and the Caledonian Society concert tonight—
damn her luck with all that mess of haggis and bagpipes
round her. On second thoughts I'll send her to the inquest
and keep her out of Uncle John's way as much as possible.
Right, to the barricades, *mes enfants!*"

As Davidson and Seymour filed out the apprentice from
the works pushed his way into the room. "Three pages to
read, Mr. Crompton, and Mr. Franks wants to know when he
can have the front page lead intro."

"That is a very good question," Crompton said solemnly.
"Tell Mr. Franks I'll think about it."

He slammed the door after the lad, and threw the page
proofs on a side table. He sat down at his own desk and took
a dozen sheets of copy paper from a pigeon-hole. He took
time to sharpen his pencil, and then scratched his head with
the blunt end, and grunted. Something nicely restrained. A
straightforward statement to the effect that Danny Moss was
due to be hanged that morning of publishing day by the chief
public hangman, Mr. Edward Jessop, at Brankley Prison,
and then a brief resume of the murder, the trial, the appeal,
and the petition that was dismissed.

The door opened. "How's the lead going, Crompton?"

"On with it now," Crompton said shortly.

"Don't be too long! Turner's waiting for the copy before
he can go on to single col."

The door closed, and Crompton told him to some-
thing-or-other off. Ten minutes later Franks, the overseer,
put his head round the door. "Got the copy yet, Johnny?"

"Another five minutes, Ted, and the old cock can have it."

"I can get the front page made up when we've got that."

Crompton swore at him, and Franks grinned and went.

Quarter of an hour later Crompton went into Edward
John's room, laid the copy beside him, and walked out again.
He went down the stairs, winked at the two girls in the par-

titioned general office, and went to a nearby café to order a large black with no sugar.

When he got back twenty minutes later there was a "see me" note on his desk. He went to Packman's room and said flatly: "You want me?"

Packman swung round in what Seymour always called his revolting chair, and flapped the Danny Moss copy up and down. "What do you call this? You've written it in the wrong tense, and it's as flat as a pancake."

"We distribute through the night, and until six in the morning," countered Crompton. "The newsagents start delivering at seven o'clock. Danny doesn't get topped until nine."

"The dam' story'll be dead when we come out next week!" said Packman.

"And if a last-minute reprieve comes through on account of his age . . . ?"

"He'll swing," said Packman. "I'll bet the paper on it."

Crompton stared through the window, to where the gilded hands on the north face of St. Gudulph's clock were slowly climbing the hill to ten o'clock. In twenty-three hours, all but a few minutes, Danny would be dead, and the story would be just as dead, only colder.

In twenty-three hours Danny would be sweating it out in the condemned cell at Brankley, with the terror of the short walk to the execution shed only a few minutes ahead of him. He might be a murderer, but he was only a kid—a kid who had taken the wrong path.

He was taking the wrong line with Packman as Danny had taken the wrong line of action with life. It didn't do to fight. There were easier ways. One of them was to temporise, to delay, to hold up the story until there wasn't time to get it in the paper. . . .

"I'll have another smack at it," he told Packman, and held out his hand for the copy.

"And for God's sake get on with it," snapped Packman. "I don't know what the hell's got into you this week."

Crompton went back to his room and dropped the sheets of copy paper one by one into the waste basket. He went to work on the page proofs.

Packman roared into the room again on his way out to lunch.

"The Moss copy, Crompton! I've got to sub it, and it has to be set, and read, and corrected! I want the front page made up by three o'clock. Old Turner'll have to change his machine again as it is."

"I don't think I want to write it," Crompton said slowly.

Packman stared at him from the doorway for a full half minute. Then he gave a deep sigh and relaxed.

"I've an idea how you feel about this case, Johnny, but this is a newspaper office, and we've no column for answering the problems of love-lorn virgins. This is a job of work, and a journalist can't afford to let sentiment rule him. Now listen; by the time I get back from lunch I shall expect that copy. I'm giving you an hour and a half to reconcile your conscience with your pay packet."

Packman was half-way down the stairs when he called back: "Oh, and you can stick in about four inches of biographical matter about Teddy Jessop!"

Crompton turned back to his desk, and a minute or so later was aware that Lisbeth Ann was laying copy beside him. "Much in it?" he asked.

"Good top of the column stuff, I think."

There was something in her voice that made him look up. She was flushed and upset.

"What's wrong?"

"Nothing. Nothing at all. Can I go for lunch now?"

Crompton nodded. He waited until she was clear of the building, and then ambled to the reporters' room. Seymour was alone, flogging an obsolete typewriter that for many years had refused to give up and die.

"What's wrong with the bint this time, Bill?" he asked.

The lad grinned. "I don't know all of it, but when I came in five minutes ago Harry boy had a red mark across his face, and Lisbeth Ann was tidying her blouse."

"Oh God! Hasn't Davidson got more sense than to start that lark!" complained Crompton.

"He's keen on her—and she has eyes only for the man in the next room," said Seymour, simulating bashfulness.

"Next room?" queried Crompton. "Don't talk so darned silly, or I'll clip your earole!"

"Actually," said Seymour, "it gets a bit binding in here. It's nothing but talk of Johnny from morning till night. If I didn't like you I could almost wish you'd get fired. But me—I like you nearly as much as Lisbeth Ann does! Would you care to come to the play with me tonight?"

Crompton flicked his right ear and stalked from the room. Lot of damned nonsense! A kid of her age got these silly notions, but thank goodness they soon wore off.

He went up St. Gudulph's Gate to the Golden Falcon, which stood on the corner of the Gate and the Market Square. He nodded to various acquaintances on his way to the lounge bar, where he began to drink steadily and deliberately.

The first half hour of his liquid lunch was agreeable, and then every time he looked in his tankard he began to see Danny Moss, trussed and hooded, standing on the trap in the shed at Brankley. His stomach churned, so he went to the nearest milk bar, drank a pint of cold milk, and swallowed five aspirin tablets. His stomach resumed an even keel, and he went back to the office, uncovered his typewriter, and lifted it from the side table to his desk.

When Packman came in Crompton handed him a new wad of copy. Packman took it to his room and came back straight away.

"Look, is this stuff what I want?"

"I hope so," said Crompton.

"Well, sub it and put it down in the case-room. I'm submerged with copy in there. I'm glad to see you thought twice about writing it!"

Crompton smothered a grin and went down to the case-room, where he subbed the copy and handed it to Franks. "That's the Moss dirt, Ted."

"Thought I was never going to see the ruddy stuff. Thanks, Johnny."

Crompton was in a remarkably good temper all afternoon, and walked around with the smug expression of a cat that had stolen a basin of cream and had not been detected. He, Packman, Seymour were busy with proofs all through until tea-time, and Lisbeth Ann and Davidson were out on jobs.

They took a short tea-break, and settled in again to the job of getting the paper to bed. Later, Seymour went to his play, Lisbeth Ann to her night job, and Davidson had simply not returned from the Young Farmers' Club assignment.

Crompton slipped to a nearby tavern for a livener, and on his return ran into Packman on the corridor. Packman waved a page proof at him, the proof of the front page.

"Thought I shouldn't notice it until it was too late, eh?" he blasted out. "Tamest story you could write about Danny Moss, eh? Timed it, didn't you? Gave it to me when you knew I should have to send it down without reading it! I've shot better journalists! You talk about ethics, and that's as far as it gets!"

"I—" began Crompton, but Packman cut him short.

"Call yourself a writer into the bargain, too!" Packman raved on. "You couldn't write insets for parish magazines! I'll show you how to write the Danny Moss story. You should join up with Charlie Carrington! Writing imaginary crime stories is all the pair of you are good for. Ethical considerations, you say! Squeamish, that's the word, Mister Crompton. I must have the worst staff of bloody incompetents in the country—and you're the worst of a bad staff!"

It was then Johnny Crompton hit him. He hit him square on the point of the jaw. Edward John's eyes went crossed, his knees buckled, and he slid down the door frame to the floor, to stay there, out cold. Crompton snatched the fallen proof from the floor, held it against the wall while he initialled it as correct, and took it down to the case-room to Franks.

"You can start running after the break, Ted," he said.

He left the premises, and went across to the Golden Falcon.

3
THE STORYTELLER'S TALE

IT WAS LATER the same evening, as he afterwards told the police, that Charlie Carrington, his day's work done, walked steadily down town, paused at the entrance to St. Gudulph's Gate, decided not to go down to the *News* office, and turned into the Golden Falcon, where he met Johnny Crompton. The five-star hotel was the rendezvous of the town's reporters. In addition to the *Borough News*, the town also carried the burden of the district branch offices of two county papers, the *Burnham Morning Courier*, and the *Burnham Evening Argus*, to each of which was attached one senior and one junior reporter. It was also known for the plain-clothes men to call at the Falcon at odd times, either for a drink or "to see if anyone is in", which meant they were looking for a wrongdoer or an informer. Carrington had also been known to pick up ideas for stories in the saloon bar.

All four district men were with Crompton, who moved forward to greet Carrington as he walked in.

"Know what Edward John's doing with the Moss story?" he asked without preamble.

"I'll take a guess at thirty-six-point caps over four cols," said Carrington.

"Forty-eight, over the lot," said Crompton. "The legend reads *Young thug's career ends*, and we come out with that an hour and a half before Danny gets topped. I could be sick!"

Carrington nodded his sympathy.

"He's still got the front page open—I think," continued Crompton. "Played hell about it all day. Nothing I could do would suit him. I got one version actually in the page, and he ripped it out again, so I told him to go to hell and do it himself. He said he would."

Carrington signalled George, the waiter, for two of the usual, and offered Crompton a smoke.

"Find it difficult to get another job?" he asked.

Crompton shrugged. "I doubt it. I know my job. It's just that I suffer from ethics. I'll have to be inoculated against them."

Carrington tut-tutted. He knew Johnny Crompton pretty well. He was a young man who could write well, and also drink well when he was in the mood, which admittedly was not often. He was also too sensitive.

The waiter came back with the drinks, and Crompton immediately lowered the level of his tankard by two inches. "Staying here for a while, Charlie?" he asked.

"May as well," said Carrington. "I've written all I intend to write for today, and Cora's out at some female dog-hanging or other. Actually, I was on my way down to the office, and pulled in here to decide whether it was safe for me to show my nose, knowing E.J.'s temper."

Crompton looked almost sheepishly over the top of his tankard. "You know, Charlie, I think I'll go back and write the copy for him, and later tell the old swine what I think of him. Follow the old Army style—do the job first, and then moan like the clappers. You know how it is with copy . . . ? Not doing it makes you feel as uncomfortable as if you've parted your hair on the wrong side of your head. Actually, it's all in the brain, and only needs pushing across the typer."

"Habit," said Carrington. "That's what it is, Johnny. Established habit tracks. It's a darned good psychological trick to break 'em down sometimes before they get topside of you. Anyway, didn't you say E.J. was writing the stuff for himself?"

"Yeah," Crompton replied shortly, "but the old so-and-so can't write, and never could. I'd hate to look at that front page in the morning if he'd had a go at it."

He emptied his tankard and put the vessel on a side table. "It's the dead hour, you know," he said as he went out.

Carrington knew all about that. On press night the pages were usually ready by eight o'clock. The page proofs were taken upstairs and laid on Packman's desk, and then everyone in the building—reporters, compositors, stonehands and machine-minder alike—adjourned to one or other of the nearby pubs for a twenty-minute break before the job of printing was undertaken. It was a small paper, and everybody turned a hand to the job, which was done on out-of-date equipment. If Packman's temper was not too bad when it was time for break, then all concerned stretched the twenty minutes to half an hour. Judging by reports, it was likely to be a short break tonight.

With Crompton on his way to the office, Carrington joined the *Courier* and *Argus* men, and together they rode the range of the normal bar topics—politics, court cases, and the odd doubtful story thrown in for luck.

Crompton was away, said Carrington, for just over a quarter of an hour. He was sure of that, for he well remembered comparing his watch with the bar clock as Johnny rejoined him.

Lisbeth Ann was tagging along behind him, and it seemed to Carrington that both of them were looking a wee bit pale round the gills, as if the strain of the atmosphere at the office were beginning to tell.

Carrington nodded briefly, and ordered a new round of drinks which included a pineapple juice for Lisbeth Ann.

"A good drink for you," commented Crompton, "but most unusual for a girl reporter. However, if that's what you want, that's what you want. Press on regardless, my girl!"

After half an hour's conversation mainly about nothing, it occurred to Carrington that the two should be back at the office by now, and so he nudged Crompton and indicated the Dutch windmill clock on the wall.

Crompton shook his head. "Not going back, Charlie. Not going back there—ever," he said under his breath.

"You wrote up Danny?"

"Packman had done it. It was in the page. Never saw him. He must have cleared off for a drink. Leave the stuff, I say. I'll tell everybody that Johnny Crompton—hic—Johnny Crompton didn't write that muck!"

Carrington let the matter drop. It wasn't his business, anyway, and Edward John—in spite of Crompton's assertion—was quite capable of doing everything from writing the copy to setting it in type and putting the paper to bed. He could print it if necessary. Carrington dismissed the matter from his mind, and ordered a further round of drinks. It was then ten minutes to nine.

At nine o'clock Detective Sergeant Harry Joynson walked in, nodded all round, and went out again.

Crompton chose the moment to bang his tankard down heavily and noisily demand more beer for all.

"Wonder who Harry's looking for?" murmured Morgan, the *Argus* senior.

Crompton shrugged. "Luscious Lulu probably pinched another Dr. Barnado box and gone to some other pub to spend the proceeds. Not to worry, old boy. It's a horrible world."

At a quarter-past nine Joynson again appeared. This time he beckoned Carrington into the lounge passage. "How long has Johnny been with you, Charlie?"

"Why?" asked Carrington.

"Yours not to ask questions, old man. How long has he been here?"

"He was here when I came in at twenty to eight."

"Sure of that?"

"Dead certain."

"You saw him yourself?"

"Of course," replied Carrington.

"You can swear you saw him in here at twenty to eight?" persisted Joynson.

"I wear glasses only for close work like tatting and embroidery."

Joynson touched Carrington's arm in a gesture of thanks, and hurried away. Carrington flag-wagged Crompton to join him in a walk to the toilets.

"Harry-boy wanted to know how long you have been here. I told him twenty to eight."

"Thanks, Charlie," said Crompton. He offered no further explanation of Joynson's interest in him until they were re-entering the lounge, when he said: "I socked him—hard."

"You must have the next drink on me," said Carrington. He added: "Lisbeth Ann wasn't present?"

"No, I met her on the way back from the Caledonian Society Highland Games or whatever they were doing, and turned her back. I decided that Uncle John would not be in a presentable state nor a good temper when he came round."

"You knocked him *out*?" asked Carrington.

"Stone cold out," said Crompton. "He was a lovely sight, Charlie. He—hic—looked like an innocent baby sitting there—"

"Sitting where?"

"On the corridor floor, Charlie, with his back against the door frame. His fat cheeks were as pink as a baby's bassinette, and the fat on his neck was just like a—hic—Venetian blind. There was a beautiful bruise forming on his chin, and the blood was running down the back of his head—"

Carrington pushed him into an alcove, and hurriedly asked: "Where the hell did the blood come from?"

"His head, of course! From where his head hit the door frame after my fist had clocked him on the point of the jaw, and—"

"Oh, my Gawd!" groaned Carrington.

"Charlie," said Crompton. "You don't think I hit poor Uncle John too hard, do you?"

"We'll pray for fine weather," said the practical and thoroughly sober Carrington. "You'll probably get a gold medal from the Union, so why worry? Every reporter in the country must have wanted to sock his editor at some time or other. You, being unique, have done it. My Gawd!"

Morgan edged towards them as they strolled as nonchalantly as they could towards the journalistic group. He whispered from the corner of his mouth, with his right hand held edgewise to his cheek as a screen to prevent anyone else hearing. It was a mannerism developed from continually making uncomplimentary remarks about the magistrates during court hearings.

"I'm off!" he said dramatically. "Spicer's been down from the warehouse and had a word with Okky."

Spicer was a detective sergeant; the warehouse was the unofficial name for borough police headquarters; and Okky was mine host of the Falcon, Hugh O'Connor.

Morgan, and Newnes of the *Courier*, did the vanishing act, leaving their juniors to keep eyes open for anything else unusual that might happen.

Lisbeth Ann, still clutching her glass of pineapple juice, looked pleadingly into Crompton's now wavering eyeballs. "Lay off it, Johnny. Please!"

His answer was to put his tankard on the counter and sarcastically ask Sally, the barmaid, for a half of Alka-Seltzer.

She supplied it, too, and told him in definite terms that it was the strongest drink he was getting for the rest of *that* evening session.

Then Bowden came on the scene, Detective Chief Superintendent Murray Bowden, chief of the borough C.I.D. He wanted a private word with Carrington, and escorted him to O'Connor's private office, obviously bespoke.

He was tall, and broad, and had dark and deep-set eyes which he had trained, right from his early days in the Force, to stare unblinkingly at a witness or a suspect in such a manner as to intimate that he Knew All About It, and there was no point in trying to stall or lie. It was such an ingrained habit that he used it on the innocent as well as the suspected, but Carrington knew the counter-measure prescribed by the Yogi, and caused Bowden to look down at his own boots.

"Er—there's bad news for Miss Grosvenor, for Lisbeth Ann," Bowden said reluctantly. "One of the linotype operators has found Mr. Packman as dead as mutton."

Carrington took a deep breath, and blew it out in a great gust. Then he said: "How?"

Bowden's neck came out of his size seventeen collar like that of a tortoise that has scented a fresh lettuce.

"Now there's a thing!" he said. "Why didn't you ask *when*?"

"As a writer of what you rudely call whodunits I'm primarily interested in *how*," Carrington replied. "It was the Red Indian giving the girl a lift in his canoe who said he knew how, but not when."

"You knew he was dead!" Bowden challenged him.

Carrington shook his head.

"No, I didn't, Bowden, but I'm not so surprised as to be shocked. I know he was alive when I joined Johnny Crompton at twenty to eight, and I have not moved from the house since, but at the risk of sounding like Sherlock Holmes I guessed something serious was astir. Two of your boys have been popping in and out, and one asked questions about Johnny's comings and goings, so I reckon I was justified in thinking that something was *up*. You merely confirmed my suspicions."

"You merely confirm mine as well," snorted Bowden. "You're almost convincing, but not quite. We'll talk about it later."

Bowden looked Carrington over for a few moments, and then said brusquely: "You've got imagination if you haven't got brains. Perhaps you'd better come and have a look at him before we take him down. He might give you an idea—and I rather fancy we're going to need some."

"Take him down, did you say?"

Bowden nodded slowly. "I said that, Mr. Carrington. We'll go out the other way. I don't want to disturb Miss Grosvenor and Mr. Crompton yet—particularly Mr. Crompton."

They left the Falcon by the Market Square entrance, and walked round the block and down St. Gudulph's Gate. As they walked Carrington asked: "Take him down, you said?"

"At first sight it looks as if somebody has been trying to crucify him. He ain't pretty to look at—not that he ever was much of an oil painting. What writer is?"

"As a policeman, you should be a good judge of ugliness," retorted Carrington, but he grew more and more reluctant to view the dead Packman as they neared the office on the left side of the Gate, and dead opposite the church.

Bowden shooed a constable from the doorway, and three of his men, including a photographer, backed to make way for him as he entered the building.

At one time the office had been one large room, but a right-angled partition had been built so that it enclosed a new and smaller office, and left a passageway running round it to the foot of the stairs. The partition was on the right as the door was opened. It was ceiling high, and from four feet above the floor it was set with one-foot squares of hammered glass. In the middle of the two bottom rows of panes was a wide pigeon hole, fitted with a shutter that could be moved up and down in copper-lined rebates by the two girls who occupied the office and dealt with advertising and general business.

The head of Edward John Packman was protruding through the hole, and the shutter was hard down on his neck. A pane on either side had been broken, and one of his hands pushed through each. His eyes and mouth were half open, and he was obviously very dead.

"Exhibit One," said Bowden with a showman-like wave of a large hand.

After Carrington had been outside to the gutter he returned somewhat shakily to ask a question.

"When—when did this happen?"

Bowden stuck a finger up behind his head to suggest a Red Indian feather. "You now wish to know when. Me know but not tell."

"To hell with you," snapped Carrington. He took a deep breath to steady his nerves, and then asked: "How?"

Bowden took his wrist and led him round the corner of the partition to the office door, which faced the foot of the stairs.

Packman's body was stretched over the narrow service counter. There was a bloody mess between his shoulder blades, and in the middle of it was the haft of a silver paper-knife.

Carrington reached for the support of the door frame. "Poor old E.J.," he gulped.

Bowden patted him in a fatherly manner. "Get a hold on yourself, Mister Murder Writer! Break the news to Johnny Crompton—if he doesn't know more about it already than we do, and then tell Lisbeth Ann. Break it as gently to her as you can, or I'll screw your head from your shoulders over a long period of time."

Carrington forced himself to take another look at Packman's messy remains. "A knife," he said. "It wasn't Johnny Crompton, thank God!"

"I'll decide who it was and who it wasn't," said Bowden. "You get moving, because I'm rather interested in the possible reactions of certain people. Then come back here. I may want you!"

At the Falcon, Carrington decided to break the news to both Lisbeth Ann and Crompton at one telling. Lisbeth Ann stared at him for a few moments and then slid gently to the heavily carpeted floor.

Carrington and Crompton looked at each other across the gap she had left.

"How did he die?" asked Crompton.

"It was a silver paper-knife through the back," replied Carrington. "You've nothing to worry about, Johnny—although I'd be prepared for trouble from Murray Bowden."

"I am," Crompton said grimly.

They got Lisbeth Ann to her feet, and she opened her eyes and smiled wanly at them. "I didn't like Uncle John, but it was a shock to hear he'd gone . . . like that. I'll be all right now, Mr. Carrington. Honest, I will!"

Crompton turned to the barmaid and ordered two tomato juices in one glass. He drank the lot at one gulp, and nodded to Carrington.

"You'll have to help me to put the paper to bed now, Charlie," he said.

His mouth twitched ironically.

"We'll take Danny Moss off the front page, and put Edward John in his place, with a nice forty-eight-point Century head across the whole lot. That's only justice, isn't it? He's news now, and we must follow the policy of the paper. *Even your own granny*, you know."

"You're a darned sight worse than he was," grunted Carrington.

"I'm a reporter," Crompton said grimly, "and we've a story on our own doorstep—or inside it! When we get to the office I want you to phone Bill Seymour at the Civic Hall, and tell him to come straight in. Then we have to locate Davidson as well, and get him."

"What about Lisbeth Ann?" asked Carrington. "Shall I ring Cora, and ask her to fetch her?"

"I'll be all right," protested Lisbeth Ann. "I want to help."

"You can ring Cora, and tell her to prepare for a visitor," said Crompton, "but she ain't going home yet, my friend. It's her paper now, and she's a reporter, and we can't let sentiment stand in the way of a good front page. It'll be every hand to the pumps now—and we'll have the tecs getting under our feet for days." Carrington looked at Lisbeth Ann. She was pale, and unsteady on her feet, and her fingers were trembling. "Well?" he said.

"I'm going back to the office with Johnny!"

Carrington grimaced. "Looks as if you'll make one, after all. Even your own granny, Lisbeth Ann!"

4
NOW LYING DEAD

NOBODY IS INDISPENSABLE, and everyone is expendable, in the world of journalism, and the job of rewriting and re-making the front page of the *Borough News* went on that night as if Edward John Packman, editor and manager of the paper for eighteen years, was alive and active instead of lying on the slab at the mortuary awaiting the post-mortem attentions of Mr. James Collingwood Baxter, the Home Office pathologist, who was motoring through the night from his Birmingham home.

Murray Bowden had caused Edward John's body to be removed expeditiously before Lisbeth Ann arrived at the office, and had given Crompton and all others concerned strict instructions regarding where they could and could not go in the building. The general office downstairs was out of bounds, and so was the section of passageway that led to the front door. The remaining part of the passageway, from the foot of the stairs to the works door, which faced the front door, was useable, but not the door itself, for Bowden was having it removed and taken to headquarters for examination by the fingerprint experts. All entrance to and exit from the building must be by the works door in the yard at the side of the block. "Otherwise," he said, "you can go where you like and do as you wish."

"Thanks for nothing," said Davidson, who had turned up of his own accord. "In case of emergency, such as the works getting on fire, we can leave by the landing window, crawl up and down the north-light roof of the works, and drop into the field at the back."

"Do that by all means if it should be necessary," replied Bowden. He left a constable on guard inside the front door, and went back to headquarters to meet the county C.I.D. chief and the county's chief constable.

Lisbeth Ann was given the job of brewing tea for the journalistic staff, and Crompton settled down at his typewriter to knock out the preliminary story of Packman's death.

Carrington meanwhile ambled round the works asking questions. After a time he went upstairs and let himself into Crompton's room. Crompton knew he was there, but was too busy to acknowledge him. After a few moments he said to Carrington: "You can take the intro down to Turner's machine for me if you please, Charlie."

Carrington picked up the first folio of the copy and began to read it aloud: *"At half-past eight last night Edward John Packman, for eighteen years the editor of the* Carrbank Borough News, *was murdered . . ."*

He laid the folio of copy down and opened his cigarette packet. He leaned over and pushed a cigarette between Crompton's lips, flipped one into the corner of his own mouth, and then flicked his cigarette lighter. He picked up the first folio, which he had just read, held it by one corner, and put the flame of the lighter under the lower corner.

Crompton, suddenly aware of what he was doing, spun round in his chair and grabbed at the burning sheet of copy paper. "What the hell do you think you are doing, you crazy fool?"

Carrington turned away, and held the sheet clear until his fingers grew too warm to hold it, when he let it drift slowly to the floor. Then he drew the nearest chair towards him and sat across the seat with his arms folded across the back. From there he smiled sardonically at Crompton.

"You nearly created journalistic history, Johnny!"

"What the devil are you talking about?" Crompton demanded. "It may not have read very well, but it took me a full five minutes to concoct that stark intro!"

"Were you writing a confession, Johnny?"

Crompton stared. "A confession . . . ? What do you mean? What are you talking about?"

"At half-past eight last night," quoted Carrington. "Tell me, Johnny! How do you know it was at half past eight?"

Crompton continued to stare, wordlessly.

Carrington swung himself free of the chair and walked to the door. "You know, Johnny, I'm in for a difficult time. One of the few human traits I admire is loyalty—and one's loyalties can be strained at times. During the past years I have received multitudinous favours from our revered county chief of detectives, Reginald Arthur Crossley, and if he asks any favours in return I shall be a skunk if I refuse him. On the other hand, I owe a great deal to this office—even to Edward John. You do see what I mean, Johnny?"

Crompton half-rose from his chair. "You don't think that—that . . ."

"All I know is that at half-past eight you were not with me in the Falcon. I've lied for you once tonight, but then I thought you'd done nothing worse than sock E.J. on the jaw and lay him out. For Christ's sake be careful in the next few days, Johnny! And for Lisbeth Ann's sake, too."

"Why for Lisbeth Ann?" asked Crompton.

Carrington raised his eyes to the ceiling. "Lord, the man is also blind."

He went to the reporters' room, and there found Davidson and Seymour helplessly watching Lisbeth Ann, who was sitting white-faced and apparently empty-minded in a corner of the room.

Davidson pushed him out to the corridor. "Can't you do something about her, Charlie? Bowden's had her down at the mortuary, identifying E.J."

"He couldn't do anything else," replied Carrington. "We have to be fair to the man. She's the only surviving relative. I'll ring Cora and ask her to bring the car down and take the kid back. Up to now it's been a rough night for her, and I'm afraid there's as bad to come."

"How come?"

Carrington shook himself from a reverie. "Hm? How come? Well, it is murder, you know, and there's the inquest, eventual committal, and assize."

"You mean Bowden knows who did it?"

"Bowden knows? Oh no, I didn't say that," replied Carrington. He shook himself. "Somebody did it, and the police are not mugs. The days of the Bow Street Runners have gone. They'll get him eventually, Harry, so the girl's in for a rough time. Still, I must phone Cora."

Crompton's door was flung open, and he appeared in his shirt sleeves, and with a cigarette hanging from a corner of his lips. "Davidson! Oh, you're there, Harry! Take this stuff down to the case-room, and tell Turner I'll have the intro down soon. Damned if I can get the thing to come as I want it. Oh, and knock out a six-col head for the story, and a three-line double col second head. Don't ham it! I want it as straight as you can get it. Oh, damn, I'll have to do a panel about Danny as well. That's all he's getting—a panel. And I must ring Baxby in the morning to tip us off if there's any hitch at the prison. Here's the copy!"

He handed it over and vanished into his room.

"Seems to have got Johnny going round in circles," commented Davidson.

"There's a lot of responsibility on his shoulders now," replied Carrington, and went to the telephone.

Lisbeth Ann was handed over to the care of Carrington's wife, Crompton finished his stories and got Seymour brewing more tea, and Carrington joined Davidson in proof reading and correcting.

By half-past one in the morning the page was locked, the forme carried to the old flatbed press on which ill-natured people said *Joe Miller's Jest Book* had been printed in 1739, and there was a further break for cups of tea before the run was started.

Sometime later Carrington mentioned to Crompton the possibility of going home and getting some sleep. Crompton said he would not bother; he'd stay at the office all night, have a snooze in a chair, get breakfast at an early-opening café round the corner, and stay put until he had heard from Baxby, of the *Brankley Echo*, that no reprieve had turned up, and that Danny Moss had been hanged.

"I'll give you a prize for zeal," said Carrington, "but Charlie is going home! I'll have to walk it, too. Can't drag Cora out again at this hour of the morning, and I seem to remember that the buses have stopped running!"

He was ambling down the stairs, and through the passage to the works when a booming voice asked where he thought he was going.

Carrington put his head into the general office and smiled sleepily. "To bye-byes, Bowden! Wish you were coming?"

Bowden returned the smile. "Wish you weren't coming?"

"Hm?" murmured Carrington.

"You're coming back with me to the warehouse. Mr. Crossley would like to talk to you."

"At this time of the flipping morning?" protested Carrington. "I ain't awake, man!"

"That's the idea, isn't it?" enquired Bowden. "You've spread yourself often enough in your books about the police fetching people out of bed in the middle of the night to question them, when they aren't awake, and consequently off their guard. Now it's your turn, cock—or ours. The carriage awaits at the entrance to the drive, me lord!"

So Carrington found himself shanghaied, and delivered to Bowden's office at police headquarters. Sitting at the desk was Detective Chief Superintendent Reginald Arthur Crossley, of the county C.I.D., a fresh-complexioned man of forty-eight with close-cropped fair hair.

He grinned as Carrington was ushered in. "Got you at last, Charlie! I hope Bowden's cautioned you. Anyway, press on regardless with your business. I've enough to do here for the next half hour."

"We shan't disturb you for long, sir," Bowden said sarcastically. "Mr. Carrington will soon have told us all he knows."

"Whereas you would never even get started," retorted Carrington.

Bowden ignored the insult. "Take a pew, here. Have a smoke. . . . Now then, you and Packman recently had a row. That correct?"

"It's a leading question, and I could object to it," said Carrington, determined to be as awkward and offensive as possible. "You should ask if I saw Packman recently, and then what transpired at the interview."

"I'm asking you if you had a bloody row with him!"

"You could call it that," said Carrington.

"And with regard to what was it in aid of?" asked the exasperated detective.

"It was with regard to a matter over what I had decided to do nothing about with," replied Carrington.

Crossley looked up, hurriedly forced back a smile, and said "Charlie! Please!"

"You had a row! What was it about?" demanded Bowden.

"Call it a dispute," said Carrington. "He wanted me to wrap flowers of verbosity around many of Danny Moss's appearances in courts, and I refused. I'm no ham."

"We won't intrude personal opinions," Bowden said nastily.

"It would have been as lowering to my prestige to write that stuff as it will be to you if you have to call in New Scotland Yard to help you with a job you can't manage," replied Carrington.

Bowden grimaced after looking at his chief, and asked: "At what time did you join Crompton in the Falcon tonight?"

"I've answered that twice already," said Carrington. "It was about twenty to eight. He was there with the *Courier* and *Argus* boys. I imagine he had been there for some time, and had not just arrived."

"Twenty to eight," muttered Bowden. "Where had you been before then?"

"At home. My wife will corroborate that if you care to give her a ring."

"Wives!" sneered Bowden. "They'll back a man in anything!"

"We mustn't drag in personal experiences," said Carrington.

Bowden sighed dramatically. "We're fencing unnecessarily, and wasting time."

"You took the foils from the case, and now you don't want to play," Carrington pointed out. "There is a faint possibility that I could help you."

Crossley looked up and nodded briefly.

"I don't like amateurs interfering, thank ye," said Bowden. "We'll have enough amateur theories pouring in over the blower during the next few days—amateurs and informers with phoney evidence, without inviting you to take part."

"I wasn't suggesting that," said Carrington. "I'm in the position of knowing the office routines without being a staff member."

Bowden ran his tongue round the inside of his cheek and regarded Carrington with new interest. "There is that," he conceded.

"Trouble with you," said Carrington, "is that you don't think straight. Because I write crime stories doesn't mean that I set myself up as an amateur criminologist, any more than you profess to be a writer. We would probably drop first-class clangers if we tried to do each other's jobs. I read Moriarty, and Hans Gross, and Richard Harrison, and the rest of 'em, but I don't practice as a private eye."

Bowden perched his bulk on the edge of the table.

"I'm trying not to be suspicious, cock, but you are cramming too much baccy in the pipe of peace. Still, it's a bargain. It you'll promise not to play detectives I'll promise not to read your books!"

"Why?" Carrington asked innocently. "Can you read?"

Bowden's reply was in monosyllabic Anglo-Saxon, and as Carrington pointed out, it was a suggestion he could not carry further.

"Having got over the preliminary rounds," he added, "is there anything else you want from me in the way of information?"

"Yes. Did you stay in the lounge of the Falcon all evening?"

"I went out once."

"Ah! What for?"

"Natural reasons."

Bowden swore, and the conversation came to an end.

Crossley rose from his desk. "Will Mr. Crompton be at the office at this time of the night, Charlie?"

Carrington told him he was staying until Danny Moss was hanged.

"I'd like to meet him if you'll take me down. He may be able to assist us."

Carrington and Crossley went by police car to the *News* building, and as Crossley got out he stood on the edge of the kerb, looking up at the façade.

"Oldish?" he asked.

"Early last century," said Carrington. "In daylight you'll see two terracotta griffons perched on the gables. Packman bought them at a sale, and had them fixed up there in an attempt to give a touch of character to what you'll agree is an otherwise architecturally uninteresting building.

"The yard on the left here is the delivery entrance to the works. This green door is the only other entrance or exit the building provides. The whole of the top floor at the front is used as editorial offices, and the downstairs front is taken up by the general office, a store room, cubby-hole used for tea-mashing and toilet, and the staircase. The works behind is built on, and only one-storied."

"Thanks," said Crossley. "Now let's meet Mr. Crompton."

Crompton was mooning round in the editor's room with a cigarette drooping from his lips, and his fair hair hanging lankly over his forehead. The whole room was throbbing with the vibration of the ancient press below as it churned out the weekly twenty-thousand copies of the *Borough News*, five readers to a copy.

"I think you know each other," said Carrington.

"Crompton and I know each other by sight," said Crossley.

Crompton nodded. "How-d'ye-do, Mr. Crossley. Rotten job, isn't it? Anything I can do to help you?"

"There may be a great deal—and there may be nothing," said Crossley. "I take it you're in charge now?"

"For tonight, anyway," replied Crompton. "God knows what happens after daylight breaks and the paper's on the streets, but I shall start to get next week's issue together. A lot depends on Lisbeth Ann—Miss Grosvenor, and a lot more probably depends on the lawyers. Yes, Mr. Crossley, for a little longer I'm a big-time editor for the first time in my life—perhaps the last time, too."

Crossley picked the proof of the front page from the desk, and read aloud the black-letter panel: *"Danny Moss, 19-year-old carpenter's apprentice, sentenced to death at Burnham Assizes for the murder of his xx-year-old sweetheart, Stella Wellesley, was executed at Brankley Prison this morning. The executioner was Edward Jessop."*

He glanced at Crompton, who wrinkled his nose in a gesture of distaste.

"That caused some of the trouble, didn't it?" Crossley asked quietly.

"Opinion isn't evidence, but I'm inclined to believe it caused all the trouble," replied Crompton.

"Tell me why you think that, Mr. Crompton."

Crompton shook his head. "Opinion isn't evidence any more than is hearsay, Super. It would not be fair for me to comment."

"There was an air of disagreement in the office yesterday?"

"It was a day of days," Crompton said flatly. He stubbed his cigarette, and lit another. "You might say it was one of those days—but then, it was quite a week if it comes to that!"

"You could perhaps help me a lot by telling me about it," suggested Crossley, ever the diplomat. "I'm not asking for opinions, but for the facts of the day. You could do that?"

Crompton pulled two chairs forward. "Might as well be comfortable, Super."

Crossley brought a hand down sharply on Crompton's right hand as it gripped the top rail of the chair.

"You've surely bruised your knuckle, Mr. Crompton!"

Crompton swallowed his smoke, and coughed for a few moments. Then he said: "Sorry! Yes, I knocked them."

"Newish injury, I should say," Crossley murmured softly. "The bruises are only just coming out."

"Yes, I did them only a few hours ago while rushing round to get the paper finished."

"Coincidence is a remarkable factor in life," said Crossley. "There was a bruise on Mr. Packman's jaw when I saw his body at the mortuary. . . ."

He looked straight into Crompton's eyes, and smiled. Crompton stared him back for a short space of time, and then said: "They probably match, Super! I socked him earlier this evening."

"Ah!" sighed Crossley. "My old friend Knollis—who incidentally retired from the Yard on the 13th of August this year—was fond of quoting Voltaire to me. That cynical old philosopher was apparently of the opinion that coincidence is always the seen result of an unknown cause, and *Knollis* used to say that if you persisted the cause could always be found. It was just a matter of patience, and patience, and patience. . . ."

He smiled again at Crompton. "Perhaps you would care to tell me why you socked Mr. Packman . . . ?"

"So what? Why not?" said Crompton, and told Crossley how long the row had been blowing up, how it had started, and why he socked Packman when he did.

It took him ten minutes, and when the recital was over Crossley nodded slowly as if going over the points in his own mind.

"And that was the last time you saw Mr. Packman, when you left him in a semi-conscious position in the corridor outside the door of this room."

"Yes," said Crompton.

"You swept across to the Falcon for a drink, and stayed there."

"Yes."

"And you were with one or the other of your journalistic friends, in the Falcon, all the evening."

"Yes," said Crompton for the third time, clinching statements that he knew were not intended as questions, but reiterated statements of fact.

Crossley gave him a disarming smile. "You must forgive me if I am tiresome, but I have been in Carrbank only a short time, and have not had chance to check with Inspector Bowden on whatever facts he may have obtained."

"I'm trying to help," Crompton said flatly.

"Of course you are," said Crossley, "and you are so obviously very tired that I feel guilty of making myself a nuisance to you."

He paused, and ran a hand round his chin.

"There is a point, Mr. Crompton. I have been told that it is the practice for a constable from the Borough office to call here on Thursday evenings for six copies of your paper which help the night staff at the police station to avoid boredom—or maybe they are looking for their own names in the paper. That is so?"

"Oh, yes," Crompton agreed.

"Now Inspector Bowden did say something to me about a constable being sent along this evening in the usual way. Knowing the works staff were having break in nearby pubs he stood near the front door, waiting until they came back and began the run. While doing so he—unless he was mistaken—saw you hurry from the yard and go across the road to another pub called, I believe, the Ring o' Bells."

Crossley smiled again at Crompton. He leaned over and patted his knee. "Still, we can talk about that tomorrow, can't we? Or should I say later in the day?"

He rose from his chair, smiled at Carrington, and left them without another word.

Crompton sucked a knuckle, and squinted at Carrington over the top of his hand.

"Charlie, I'm in a ruddy mess, I think," he said.

Carrington grimaced and nodded slowly. "At the moment I wouldn't regard you as a good betting prospect, Johnny, but even so you aren't in the unfortunate position of Edward John!"

And at that moment, at the corporation mortuary, Mr. James Collingwood Baxter, Home Office pathologist, was alternately eating ham sandwiches, and exploring Edward John's anatomy with surgical instruments delicately manipulated by rubber-gloved hands.

5
DEATH OF INNOCENT SLEEP

BY THREE O'CLOCK in the morning the last of the delivery vans was away, and the members of the works staff making their way to their homes in various parts of the town. Finally, only Crompton and the fed-up constable on duty in the general office were left in the building. Crompton loosed his tie, slipped his feet from his brown shoes, switched off the light, and after several shufflings arranged himself in something like comfort in his chair, with his feet up on another, and went to sleep. He went out like a light.

At half-past four he was shaken from his sleep, and looked blearily up to see Crossley smiling down at him. Murray Bowden was standing behind him, heavy-eyed.

Crompton blinked. "As I was saying, I socked him and—oh glory, my mouth's as dry as a brick kiln. If I can find my matches I'll brew a pot of tea, and then I'll tell you about the row over Danny Moss. . . ." Crompton swung his feet to the floor, and eased himself into an upright position. He ran his hands through his tousled fair hair, and then stared at Crossley for a few seconds before giving him a wry smile. "We've done all that, haven't we?"

"Yes, Mr. Crompton," said Crossley, "we've done all that. You'd like a cup of tea? Perhaps we'll all have one."

He turned to Bowden. "Ask the constable to busy himself with the gas ring and kettle, will you? He is to have a cup with us, of course!"

Bowden plodded to the head of the stairs and bawled down them.

"I'm sorry to disturb you like this," Crossley apologised. "In a way you're a key man in our investigation. You know so much more than we do about the paper, and the building, and the people who work in it."

Crompton eyed him suspiciously, and made desperate efforts to shake the sleep from his eyes, and to encourage his heart to pump more blood to his brain. It was very obviously going to be necessary for it to work extremely well during the coming questioning session. There were two of them to contend with into the bargain. . . .

"At what time will the other members arrive?" asked Crossley.

"Ten, without fail—it's pay morning."

"Now you were telling me about going across to the Ring o' Bells, Mr. Crompton," Crossley said suavely.

Crompton buttoned his shirt neck, and tightened the knot in his tie. He grinned at the detective and said: "Oh no, I wasn't, Mr. Crossley. I'm not so deeply asleep even at—"

He glanced at his wrist watch, lying on the desk.

"—at twenty to five."

Crossley turned to Bowden. "Didn't you say that the constable saw Mr. Crompton leave the building?"

"Mornington says he was waiting for the men to come back from the pubs, and he saw Crompton almost run from the yard, and dash into the Bells as if it was a minute off closing time. Those were his actual words."

"Why did you dash like that into the pub, Mr. Crompton?" asked Crossley.

"For a drink, Mr. Crossley."

"I should have thought you'd taken all you could carry at the Falcon, by what I heard," Bowden grunted.

"Variety is the spice of life, Bowden. Different breweries."

"Now quit stalling," Bowden warned him. "Mornington saw you leave the building!"

"Mornington did not!"

"You are denying the constable's evidence?" murmured Crossley.

Crompton's brain was responding admirably to his call for a rapid awakening, and as he slid his shoes on he said: "Mornington may have seen me leave the yard and cross to the Bells."

"Well?" said Bowden truculently.

"You may have worked the police spiv's fast one by trying to catch me out when you thought I was out on my feet, Bowden," said Crompton, "but before you start that lark just get your own evidence straight. *Mornington did not see me leave the building.* He saw me leave the yard, and that is a very different matter. Mornington may see a ragged man leaving St. Gudulph's Church, but he must not assume that he's been robbing the poor box!"

Crossley interposed. "The other members of the staff, Mr. Crompton? Can you tell me where each of them were yesterday? Is that possible?"

"You're not so dim, Mr. Crossley," returned Crompton. "The diary's on the desk there. Help yourself while I buckle my shoes."

Bowden muttered something under his breath, so Crompton turned to him. "Listen, chum! If you intend to charge me, then get on with it. Utter the usual caution, don't forget Judges' Rules, and be careful how you put down your feet, for if you tread on the Press without justification you're in for as much trouble as any man who shoots a copper!"

"Why should Mr. Bowden think of charging you?" Crossley asked urbanely.

"Because he's got that kind of mind," returned Crompton. "It doesn't take him very far, so he likes to get off before the last stop. Everyone else was at break; I was the only member of the staff seen in the vicinity, and so two and two make five according to Bowden's standard of intelligence."

"Now steady . . . !" warned Bowden.

The constable put his head inside the door. "How shall I bring the tea up, sir? I can't find a tray."

"Bring the pot," said Crompton, "and we'll suck it through the spout. Ever tried carrying a cup in each hand, and making two trips? In fact you can make a third trip—down the stairs!"

"Getting rattled, eh?" said Bowden. "Anyway, if, as you say, you did not leave the building when Mornington saw you not coming from it, do you mind telling us why you approached it at all?"

"Charlie Carrington can tell you that I'd refused to do the job for Packman. Then I decided to do the job first, and then moan about it. Then I got as far as the yard, and changed my mind again. I said, 'To hell with him!' and went across to the Bells for a drink before I went back to the Falcon—"

"For a drink," said Bowden.

"I do my drinking openly, and don't slink up pub yards and have 'em pushed through the window for me to knock back in the shadows."

Crossley chuckled. "Almost sounds as if he's done town patrol, Bowden! Tell me, Mr. Crompton, were all these night jobs done?"

"There'll be hell to pay if they weren't," Crompton assured him.

"You'll have proof?"

"Oh yes, when they come in they'll either have the copy ready, or will get down to writing it up."

"Yes, of course," said Crossley. "By the way, when you left the Ring o' Bells, did you meet Miss Grosvenor outside, or when on your way back to the Falcon?"

"She was standing outside the Gate entrance to the Falcon. I rather fancied that she wanted to join the boys, but she's a bit shy yet of going in unaccompanied. She *said* she was on her way here to throw her notebook in, but I took that with a pinch of salt. It didn't matter a darn whether she brought it in last night or not providing the job was done."

"And was it?"

"Eh?" asked Crompton.

"I asked if the job was done."

Crompton shrugged. "As I said before, it had better be done, or I'll shake the feathers from her."

"Poor little bird!" said Crossley.

"She's a reporter, and there's no sentiment in this game, Super! You should know that. The paper comes first, before anything."

"The paper, and its reputation, Mr. Crompton," said Crossley. "The paper is something of an abstract ideal, isn't it? You journalists are in some ways like show people, and circus people. You place an importance on the paper that is greater than its true worth. The show must go on, the paper must come out. Does that ideal mean a very great deal to you?"

"It means everything, Mr. Crossley."

"My paper, right or wrong?"

"More or less the idea, yes."

"Even if that paper should be a bad paper?"

Crompton grimaced. "Well, there are bad papers, but journalists still stick to them, and work their guts out for them."

"So that even if the *Borough News* was a—shall we say a stinker?—you would still fight for it tooth and nail?"

"Yes," Crompton said flatly.

"It could have been a better paper, Mr. Crompton? I have heard that it was known in town as *Packman's Pillory*, and that readers did not like all of it, and some did not like it at all, and yet it had a large circulation because there was no competitive paper. Is that correct?"

"I have heard," said Crompton, "that many policemen criticise the police force, and its methods, hours of duty, rates of pay, and system of promotion."

Crossley nodded soberly. "I see your point, Mr. Crompton. We have our loyalties, and they cannot be shaken. We criticise internally, but do not let the general public know of it. We wash our dirty linen in private. Is that it?"

"I think so," Crompton said cautiously.

"Tell me, Mr. Crompton; now that Mr. Packman has been removed from the editorship, and assuming that you step into his shoes, how would you improve the paper?"

"Gently scan thy brother man, still gentler sister woman," quoted Crompton.

"You agree with the general criticism hereabouts, that Mr. Packman went too far with his publish-and-be-damned policy?"

"Ye-es, I do."

"His policy offended your ethical sense?"

"Yes."

"So you stabbed him in the back with his own paper-knife, and then pushed his head and hands through the windows of his own pillory!"

"Why, damn you!" shouted Crompton.

"Watch him, Bowden!" Crossley said quickly. Crompton drew his arm back to punch Bowden between the eyes, and then paused for a second, and let his arms fall by his side. He flopped into his chair and flung his arms loosely over the arms.

"You dirty, two-faced skunk!" he said quietly. "You should join the Diplomatic Corps of some Communistic state!"

"I have my job to do," Crossley said smoothly.

"And I have mine to do—and I'll plaster the pair of you across the front page of the *News* next week if it's the last thing I do!"

"It probably will be," said Bowden.

Crompton lolled back in the chair. "Listen to me! I did not kill Packman. I don't know who did kill Packman! Until a few moments ago I didn't even care who killed Packman. Now I do care! I'll find out who did it, and then I'll ram the fact down your throats and make sure that every editor in Fleet Street knows it before you do. Now get out!"

"I've brought the tea," said a plaintive voice from the doorway. "I found a box lid that makes quite a good tray, sir."

Crompton burst out laughing.

"That's the climax! Inventive genius of the police overcomes all obstacles! Policeman makes tray from shoebox lid! What a wonderful head for a story!"

Crossley took the tray from the constable and held it under Crompton's nose. "Have a cup!"

"For two pins I'd tell you where to push it," said Crompton, "but it smells a good cup, and so I'll accept a cup of the *Borough News* tea, Superintendent Crossley." He took the tea and sipped it slowly. Crossley and Bowden also drank slowly, and watched Crompton covertly.

"You've gone very quiet," Crossley said after a time.

Crompton nodded. "I've never known whether it is a genuine Chinese axiom, or one of those invented by Charlie Chan, but I like it: the mouth of the wise man chews rice."

"There's another one," said Crossley: "he who utters truth saves suffering for his soul."

Crompton gave a wry smile. "Confucius say: many man smoke, but Fu Manchu."

"My God!" said Bowden.

"Also: man who lie on hillside with pretty girl not on level," said Crompton.

"I think we should drink up and leave Mr. Crompton," said Crossley. "He's obviously in need of sleep."

Crompton pushed his cup on the desk and threw his arms wide. "Sleep no more! Crossley does murder sleep—the innocent sleep; sleep that knits up the ravelled sleeve of care, the death of each day's life, sore labour's bath, balm of hurt minds. . . ."

He paused. "Do you know, gentlemen, I'm going to cause you to lose more sleep in the next few days, or weeks, than you've ever lost in the rest of your lives! I'm going to grind you down so small that you'll go through the holes in a pepper-pot lid! You can call here to see the rest of the staff at eleven o'clock—and you won't see them earlier if you come because we have the Friday morning conference to decide the makeup for the next issue. After that they are yours."

"And later in the week you are mine," said Bowden. "You want to play it hard—okay! But I'll get you, Crompton!"

He clumped heavily from the room and down the stairs.

Crossley stayed another minute.

"Somehow, Mr. Crompton, I feel that I'm in for a rough time between the two of you. I appreciate your attitude, and only wish you similarly appreciated mine!"

"To some extent I do, Mr. Crossley, but I never did like Bowden. The difference between you is that one is a copper, and the other a gentleman—and I would like to apologise for the offensive remarks I made."

"Thank you," said Crossley as he walked through the doorway.

Crompton followed him and called over the banisters: "I'm still going to beat you to it!"

He went to the toilet room and washed. He tugged a way through his hair with his comb, and went down the stairs to the general office.

"Hey, Hawkeye! I'm going round to Peter's Pantry for breakfast in case anyone wants to know where I am. Want any buns or sandwiches bringing back?"

"All being well, God 'elp me," said the constable, "I should be relieved in half an hour. Then it's me for breakfast and a kip."

Crompton sniffed the fresh morning air as he walked along the lower end of St. Gudulph's Gate. It was just on half-past six, and the streets were slowly coming alive with hurrying workers. He turned into the early-morning café run by a bachelor who had nothing to stay in bed for, and gave the proprietor a breezy good-morning.

"Strike, Johnny!" said Peter Gregory. "I heard you were in clink!"

"For what, my good friend?" said Crompton as Gregory pushed a cup of tea across the counter.

"Doing the old boy in."

"They're saying that already?"

"They were saying it before I closed at midnight!"

"News certainly gets around," said Crompton. "Why did I do him in? Can you tell me?"

"Some sort of a row over Danny Moss being hanged."

"That's right," said Crompton. "I stabbed him, jumped on him, and broke his neck. Then I picked him up by one leg and threw him at the wall. After that I cut him into pieces and stuffed them in the stokehold fire. And this morning there's nothing left but his brace-ends and collar-stiffeners."

"You're kidding, Johnny!"

Crompton shrugged. "That'll be the story by dinner-time, old boy! Oh, and I was raving drunk when I did it!"

Gregory said: "It must have been a rough time you had with him."

"Cock, I'm hungry! Had nothing to eat since breakfast yesterday." He suddenly paused, and added: "By God, and it's true at that. Greg! Three slices of ham, two eggs, two weiners, and a slice of spam. Into the pan, quick! I've just realised that I *am* hungry!" Gregory took a look at him, and reached for the frying pan.

"Your phone working, Greg?"

"The bill's paid—on the final demand."

As the pan began sizzling in the tiny kitchen attached to the shop, Crompton went to the telephone and dialled Carrington's number. Two minutes passed before there was an answer, and then Carrington's voice asked who the hell was that.

"Crompton! I've been up all night, so I don't see why you shouldn't stir from your virtuous couch a little earlier than usual."

"What's cooking?" asked Carrington.

Crompton chuckled. "Can you smell it from there?"

"One of us is nuts," said Carrington.

"I'm in Greg's place," explained Crompton. "He's frying eggs, ham, weiners, and spam. Haven't had a bite for twenty-three hours. Anyway, I want you to come in for the conference at ten. Things are moving. I've had the pleasure of the company of Messrs. Crossley and Bowden most of the night. They waited until I was asleep, and then lobbed in and tried to persuade me to confess for the good of my soul. I've told 'em I'm going to beat 'em to it. That was a bit big-headed, actually, but I've opened my big mouth, and I'll need some help if I'm going to pull it off."

"Count on me," said Carrington. "What d'you want? A two-thousand-word confession? I'll do it if I can have lineage rates."

"Seriously, how far are you prepared to go, Charlie?"

"To within six feet of the gates of Brankley Prison—and not another step!"

"That'll do nicely, Charlie. I want the story to get round that you are under suspicion so that Bowden et Cie keep off me for a few days while I do my own private eyeing."

"Here, steady now, Johnny!" came a plaintive voice on the wires.

"You said you'd help!"

"I know I did, but dammitall!"

"You did have a row with Packman, Charlie!"

"I'm well aware of that, but—"

"Anybody who had a row with Edward John is under suspicion!"

"Now look here, Johnny, I'll do a lot for you—"

"Thanks, Charlie," Crompton interrupted. "That's just what I expected of you! See you at ten!"

Crompton was grinning as he replaced the handset in the cradle. He put his head into Gregory's kitchen. "Hear that humorous conversation, Greg?"

"What? With this lot all talking at once?" asked Gregory, indicating the contents of the frying pan. "If you're going to start having meals like this I'm going to sterilise a dustbin lid!"

"Ruddy good job you didn't hear it," muttered Crompton. Louder, he asked for the morning papers, and following directions found them behind the counter.

He took them to a seat in the window and opened them. He glanced at the front pages of the six leading morning papers, and whistled. *Somebody* had farmed out the story of Packman's death in full measure.

"Now who the dickens . . . ?" he muttered. He put the papers aside and settled down to think. Then Gregory came with his breakfast and two cups of tea, and settled down opposite him.

"Seriously, Johnny," he said; "is there any clue to who killed the old chap?"

Johnny nodded solemnly. "The place is full of clues, Greg! The police have been in the offices all night. They've taken photos, and dusted everything for fingerprints, stripped everybody down and X-rayed them, and even looked at our credentials!"

"Go on!" said the amazed café owner.

"Fact!" said Crompton as he crammed half a weiner into his mouth. "Not only the staff, either! They even dragged our local author out of bed and brought him down."

"Mr. Carrington—the crime-story writer? Not him!"

"Him," said Crompton, sawing at his ham.

Gregory rubbed his chin. "Aye now, somebody did say in here that he'd had a row with Mr. Packman—like you did."

"True, he did," munched Crompton. "The words they used weren't fit for a reporter to hear, Greg!"

"Then it *could* have been him!"

Crompton waved a portion of egg on his fork. "Now I did not say that, Greg!"

"No. No, Johnny, you didn't say it—and I'm as discreet as any man alive. You know that, don't you?"

"If there's a more discreet man I don't know him, Greg, but don't go around saying that I said Mr. Carrington is under suspicion."

Gregory got up. "Be all right while I slip to the paper shop for a few minutes? There's something I meant mentioning to

Freddy Allsop. Won't be long! Help yourself to tea—the pot's on the stove."

Gregory tucked the lower corner of his white apron into the waist-band, and hurried from the café.

Crompton watched him go, and grinned happily. "Bowden, my friend," he said; "we're off! But poor old Charlie!"

6
THE KEY TO THE PROBLEM

Carrington arrived at the *News* office shortly before ten o'clock, and straightway coralled Crompton in his office and closed the door.

"Look, Johnny," he said; "there's one question I have to ask you. You told me you had socked Packman. I've got that fact straight. What you didn't tell me was when you did it, and I may have put your foot in the hole for you. I've had Crossley and Bowden round this morning, and I said I was under the impression that you hit him when you went across during the dead hour—and that was about quarter-past eight."

Crompton shook his head. "You got it wrong, chum. I'd already done the job when you met me in the Falcon."

"That makes a difference," said Carrington. "It means that Edward John met violence in three stages."

Crompton wrinkled his forehead. "How come, Charlie?"

"Well, Crossley always opens up when he's talking to me—although Bowden tries to stop him doing so, and if I didn't misunderstand him there were three different attacks on Edward John. First you socked him, and that was about half-seven, wasn't it? Then somebody knifed him, and that would seem to have happened about eight o'clock. And later still somebody pilloried him."

"You mean the knifing and the pillory weren't part and parcel of the same business?"

"Not, as I say, unless I misunderstood Crossley."

"That's mighty interesting," said Crompton. "Do you know, I never thought to ask what time the blokes came back from break!"

"I did that while you were writing up the new front-page copy," said Carrington. "They dribbled back between half-eight and twenty to nine. Turner told me they didn't hurry because they knew the old boy was writing up the copy."

"But it was—" began Crompton, and then said:

"I'll skip that for now."

Carrington smiled. "Edward John set the copy himself. He pulled his own proof, which didn't need correcting, and put the type in the page. He then did a page pull, and he was bending over that in the general office when he was knifed. Crossley's of the opinion that the killer was someone he knew, and that when whoever it was spoke to him he did not bother to turn away from what he was doing."

"And it was someone who had a key," added Crompton. "There are six keys. We have one each, and Franks has the sixth. That makes it look a darn sight worse for me, doesn't it, Charlie?"

"Your position at the moment is what I should regard as hot," Carrington agreed. "You and I were the only two characters in this drama who had rows with him—and I have no key."

"You're still under suspicion," said Crompton. "If Franks omitted, or forgot, to drop the latch on the works door you or anybody else could have walked straight in. Franks is the only person with a key to that door—apropos of nothing much."

Davidson lounged into the room. "Did I hear sayings about a key? If anybody's found one it'll be mine. I lost the thing early in the week, and I'm darned if I can find it."

He pulled his right trousers pocket inside out to display a hole in the lining. "Must have gone down there. I've searched the car, and my digs, and looked around where e'er I've walked, but I haven't found it. Couldn't get in last night when I got back from the cage bird do, and that's why my copy isn't written up yet." Carrington tut-tutted gently. "Now there's a thing that will interest friend Bowden! This really will put the cat among the pigeons. There's one thing, Johnny—it'll relieve some of the pressure on we two."

Crompton turned to Davidson. "Tell me, you long streak of uselessness, how the devil you got in on Wednesday night after the Rotary dinner? Your copy was on the desk when I came in yesterday morning."

"Borrowed Lisbeth Ann's," Davidson said cheerfully. "I knew Packman would play smoke if he knew a key was lost, and you're never in a good temper if copy isn't written, and so I did the obvious—borrowed one. And that is the answer to the compleat angler for information."

"Then why didn't you borrow one for last night?"

"No need, was there? I expected to be back before break, and so I could have come in by the works door. As it happened, I was waylaid, and I didn't get back until later, and the door was locked."

"You could have kicked on the front door until Edward John came to let you in!"

"I did that," said Davidson. "I did that, old boy. Nearly roused the street, but all to no avail, so I said to blazes with it and went across to the Bells for a noggin."

Crompton put a foot up on a chair and pushed his nose into Davidson's face. "There's something else you can tell me, Harry boy! Who farmed out the story to the nationals?"

"Me, of course," replied Davidson. "The lolly will go into the lineage pool, and you'll get your whack, so why beef about it?"

"I'm not concerned with the monetary angle," said Crompton.

Davidson grinned at Carrington. "Johnny's ethics coming up any minute now. They cover everything from seduction to sabotage."

"And I'm not concerned with ethics," returned Crompton. "All I'm concerned with is accuracy, and that story you pumped out was anything but accurate. You hammed the whole job, and neither Carrington nor myself come out of it with much credit. So I'm warning you! You send out any more stuff before I've okayed it, and I'll beat the daylights out of you, as big as you are."

"You may be the boss now, but you won't be soon, so you'd better get in all the bossing while you've chance," snapped Davidson.

"That won't worry me," said Crompton. "The sooner I can shake the dust of this dump from my boots the better I shall like it. And who says I won't be boss much longer, anyway?"

"I—er—I don't break confidences," Davidson replied lamely.

"Then make sure you don't get something else broken!" said Crompton. "You'd better fetch the others in for a few minutes, and then get off to Jackson's committal."

The conference was shorter than expected, for a knock on the door announced the arrival of Crossley and Bowden.

"We had to come early," said Crossley. "There are so many things to be done just now. I take it we have all the editorial staff here?"

Crompton nodded. "Those in the picture are, from left, Harry Davidson, Bill Seymour, and Miss Grosvenor. If they have anything to tell you touching the death of Edward John Packman, now lying dead, they'll only be too pleased to do so. Davidson's movements for yesterday were. . . ."

"Out on a cage-bird show last night," said Davidson. "I spent most of the day, otherwise, with the Finnerton Young Farmers' Club, striding over the good earth and things left behind by cows in an effort to raise a column and a half of copy on Virile Young England. The things I did for Packman!"

"And," added Crompton, "he has lost his office key."

"Now there's a thing indeed," said Bowden. "How, when, and why, Mr. Davidson?"

Davidson repeated his explanation.

"It could not have been taken from your pocket—stolen?" Bowden suggested.

"Dunno. The idea hadn't occurred to me. Why should anyone steal a key?"

"Perhaps to unlock a door," said Bowden. "I think we should have a conversation about this."

"I've got the committal at half-past ten," said Davidson, glancing at his watch.

"Someone else can do that, surely?" Bowden asked Crompton.

"You slip off, Bill," he said.

Crossley caught him by the arm. "Before you go, would you tell us where you were last night?"

"Watching the Fortune Players chop *Thunder Rock* to pieces and selling the bits to the audience at three-and-a-tanner a time. They ought to be charged with gaining money by false pretences."

"Nevertheless," said Crompton, "you will be kind to the so-and-so's! You got a drink out of it, didn't you?"

"Maureece, the producer, took me backstage for a bottle of light ale, and told me how to write my review. I told him what to do with the bottle, and walked back to my seat."

"Good show!" exclaimed Davidson. "You are coming up the right way, but you should have drunk the beer first, and then told him what to do with the empty bottle."

"That is what I did," replied Seymour.

"Hop it, son," said Crossley. "You're growing up like the rest of 'em."

"You'll turn into a policeman if you aren't careful," said Crompton, "and then your mum won't speak to you any more."

Bowden ignored the insult, and produced his note-book and pencil. "So Mr. Davidson was at the cage-bird show, Mr. Seymour at the play, and Miss Grosvenor at the Caledonian Society concert—or so I seem to remember. That clears those three from the list. Mr. Carrington was holding up the lounge bar at the Golden Falcon, and you, Mr. Crompton, seem to have been drifting up and down the Gate with the wind."

"I never suffer from it, Bowden."

Bowden tapped his notebook. "This key is going to complicate matters. If it's lost, that's that, and it should not affect the case. If it was stolen, then we have to start thinking again. Any ideas?"

"There's a question I'd like to ask," said Crompton. "Is it, or is it not true that on two occasions you saw Packman and asked him to pipe down on the Moss story?"

Crossley turned sharply. "Well, Bowden, did you?"

Bowden grunted. "As a matter of fact it is. He was pumping the story until the police were getting gossiped about for victimising the youth. It wasn't doing us any good, so I asked him to tame his stuff down."

"I'll bet I know what he told you!" said Davidson.

"Your first guess will be correct," said Bowden. "He was most offensive."

"And you stuck out your neck for a second dose?" Crompton asked. "You must have been het up about it!"

"You have to keep trying, you know," Bowden said in an apologetic manner. "He was just about the hardest character I've come across."

"Where were you round about half-past eight last night?" Crompton asked suddenly.

Crossley raised his eyebrows at the question. He remained silent, although he watched his inspector closely.

Bowden rubbed the back of his fleshy neck, and squinted at Crompton. He did not reply.

"Well?" snapped Crossley.

"You would ask that one!" Bowden said at last. "So far as I can make out from Baxter's preliminary report I was trying the front door of this office while our unknown friend was sticking him!"

"You intended making a third attempt to get the story watered down?" Crossley asked.

"Well, yes. You see, sir, like Crompton, I was thinking about the parents. They've had it pretty rough over the past few years, and Packman was only rubbing salt into the wounds. They're nice, humble people. . . ."

"Tell me something else," said Crompton. "Were the office lights on?"

"Yes, they were, but the glass on those front windows is painted too high up for even me to see over it, and I'm six feet and half an inch tall. How did you know I was in the Gate, Crompton?"

Crompton smiled. "I passed you. You were on the other side of the street. Now, Bowden, you can stick yourself on the list of people who quarrelled with Packman, and were in the vicinity of the office when he was killed."

"Getting tough?" commented Bowden.

"Well, I warned you."

Bowden snorted. "You can add this as well then, Mister Crompton. I don't know where Canon Tapley was last night, but he also tried to persuade Packman to pipe down on his story."

"That is news to me," said Crompton. "Mind you, he's always in and out, and we don't take much notice of him. We print his parish magazine, and the old boy does occasional articles for us, and he likes fussing editors—makes him feel that he's in Fleet Street."

Crossley returned to the conversation by asking Crompton the question Carrington had already asked. Crompton assured him that he hit Packman before he went in the Falcon for the first time, and not during the dead hour.

"That agrees with Baxter's interim report," said Crossley, "but I wanted the answer from your own mouth. Now if Miss Grosvenor would not mind leaving us . . . thank you, Miss Grosvenor . . . there is one other small point I'm sure you could clear up for us, Mr. Crompton."

"If I can—certainly."

"Very well," Crossley said in a gentle voice. "Do tell us, Mr. Crompton, how Mr. Packman was lying when you found him last night."

Crompton started. "I—I didn't say that I found him. I've never said that!"

"No, but you did find him dead when you returned with the good intention of writing the Moss copy, Mr. Crompton. You must have found him!"

"This's a turn-up for the book," commented Davidson.

"You shut up," said Crompton. Then, wearily, he said: "Okay, I found him—and panicked—and dashed off to the Bells to think things out. I didn't stay there long because I realised that Charlie would wonder where the heck I was. I went in the passage, and the barman doesn't know me, and I doubt if any of the customers knew me, so I made my heels crack back to the Falcon. As I left the Bells I saw Lisbeth Ann going back to the office, so I turned her round and took her back with me.

"I let myself in by the front door, and went straight upstairs to Packman's room. He wasn't there, so I came down again. The light was on in the general office, but if Packman had been there I should have seen him—or so I thought at that moment—through the hammered-glass panels. I looked in the works, and suddenly decided it was odd. The new copy was set, and in the page. The page needed leading out and locking up, but otherwise it was complete. The new type had been inked, so I knew a proof had been pulled of it, and also knew that Packman must be somewhere in the building.

"I knew he wasn't in the smallest room in the house, for the door was open—it's on this corridor. It wasn't often he sat down in the general office to do proofs. He preferred to stand at the service counter, which is conveniently high for the job. Anyway, I looked round the door, and saw him lying on the floor between the end of the desk and the wall of the partition. . . ."

"Lying down, you said?" Crossley murmured. "Not pilloried through the screen. But of course if that had been the case you would have seen him when you first went in the office, would you not?"

"Let's finish the story," said Crompton. "Only his legs up to his hips were visible. I bent over him and saw the handle sticking from his back. He could not possibly have had any life in him, so I left him where he was. Then I thought I heard someone move upstairs, and decided to get out. I was going to dodge out by the front door, and saw Mornington through the pane in the door, so I went back and through the works. I heard Mornington walking away from the door, and dodged out when I thought he would not see me. I knew he was merely passing the time until he could get the police copies, and would turn again at the end of the building. I evidently mistimed it, and he saw me."

Crossley pulled at his lower lip and said "Hm!" Then he smiled disarmingly at Crompton. "We can see into the matter of an official statement from you later. At the moment I'm interested in the person upstairs. You are certain there was someone there?"

"Not certain," said Crompton. "It's an old building, and I've noticed before when I've been here late at night that all kinds of creaks and groans wake up after the machines have gone to sleep."

"That is a point," said Crossley. "Still, it means that in the few minutes between you hurrying out, and the first of the other men coming back, someone lifted him and pushed his head and hands through the panes. He weighed eleven stones eight pounds, and a dead man appears to weigh more than that—he is literally a dead weight. You need to be strong to do a job like that! Once the job was done he was not likely to slip back owing to his legs and hindquarters being wedged against the edge of the desk. A most interesting case!"

"And the oddest thing about it," said Bowden, "is that one of my policemen was standing at the other side of a four-teen-inch brick wall while it was happening! He never heard the panes broken!"

"Anyway," said Crossley, "I wish you all to agree to your fingerprints being taken. The sergeant is waiting down-stairs. . . ."

When the inky session was over, Carrington excused him-self to go home and get some work done, and Crompton and Davidson alone remained in the editor's room. After a time Davidson said: "Suppose I'd better hop out to Rainley in the car and see Fanny."

Crompton grunted. "Hm? Fanny? You mean the Adams woman?"

"No, you idiot," snapped Davidson. "I mean Mistress Frances Mundeham, the cast-off floozie of the late lamented Edward John. Everybody, but everybody, knows of Fanny!"

"I don't!" Crompton said quickly. "Where does she live? Rainley?"

"Yers," said Davidson, "that sweet piece of rusticity down by the river. She lives in ye olde cottage next to St. Saviour's Church. Didn't you know about her? Honest?"

"Never come into my ken," said Crompton. "How the heck did you know of her?"

"Well now, her existence in Edward John's life was more or less a secret. She was well known all right, but not in connection with E.J. One of my hobbies is running out to rural pubs and playing darts and dominoes with the yokels—for money, and I've met E.J. and Fanny on a few occasions. She was in the habit of waiting round the corner of St. Gudulph's Court with her car, and once the paper was to bed she picked him up and off they went—to the White Swan at Rainley, or the Quintain at Netherlea, or the Turk's Head at Littleby Ferry, or—"

"We can cut out the list of country pubs," said Crompton. "You say she was cast off?"

"In the process of being, although I don't think the penny had dropped on her as yet. Edward John had let his eye fall on the widow woman who runs the Ferryman Inn half a mile below Thorpe Bridge. Tricky bit she is, too!"

"What's Fanny like?"

"Aye, now Fanny is a bit of all right as well, even though she's just turned the forty mark. She has dark hair with a silver streak in it which may or may not be natural. She looks well in sleek suits, and she certainly has a figure! A vivacious character is Fanny—I'll bet she's good fun, too!"

"I'm beginning to see why E.J. was always so polite to you, and took it out of me when you dropped clangers," said Crompton. "He was scared of you opening your trap."

"Come, come!" said Davidson. "Edward John knew that I was a proper gent, discreet and all that. Matter of fact, old boy, it would hardly have paid off if I had mentioned the affair, would it? I mean, E.J. was the man who paid the lolly every Friday morning! We were mutually respectful to each other for obvious reasons."

"There are times when I don't like you, Davidson," said Crompton.

"Well, if it comes to that I've never fallen in love with you. Too la-di-da and righteous for my liking. Talking ethics and boozing like a fish don't mix, chum. Bit of a hypocrite, aren't you? What did you do with E.J.? Knock him out so that his dicky heart gave out, and then pushed the knife in his back to make it look like someone else finished him . . . ? Was that it, Johnny boy?"

"I hit him fair and square—just like this," exclaimed Crompton. His fist flew to Davidson's jaw, and Davidson reeled back, tripped over a chair, and fell into a heap beside his late editor's desk.

Davidson grabbed the edge of the desk and helped himself to his feet, nursing his jaw with his spare hand. "You'll regret that, Crompton!"

"I regret it already," said Crompton. "You aren't worth hitting! Now listen, I'm going out to Rainley on the scooter, and if I find you've either visited Fanny after I've been, or phoned her while I'm on the way out I'll give you another pasting. What you can do while I'm out is get that cagebird show written up—results and judges and everything. I'll expect it on my desk when I get back."

"Blessed is he that expecteth nothing, because he receiveth it!" said Davidson.

Crompton met Lisbeth Ann in the corridor, a large question mark in her eyes.

"I've just pasted Mr. Davidson," said Crompton. "Any objections?"

She gave a wan smile and shook her head. "You know best, Johnny."

She touched his arm. "I'd like some advice, please."

"Will it do later? I'm just off to Rainley on a story."

"We-ell—"

Alarm showed in her blue eyes. "To Rainley? I'll be here alone!"

"The girls are downstairs, and the blokes in the works," said Crompton. Then he paused, and looked at her eyes again. "You don't want to stay with *him*!"

She shook her head. "Can I come out with you—on the back of the scooter?"

Crompton considered for a few moments. "On one condition. You take a walk round the village and feed the swans while I do the interview. It isn't one at which I'd like you to be present. Okay?"

She brightened. "Okay, Johnny! Have I time to powder my nose?"

"Meet me in the yard when you're ready," said Crompton. "By the way, did you lend Davidson your key this week? You did? Well that answers one important question, anyway. But, Lord, how many remain!"

7
MISTRESS OF THE SITUATION

RAINLEY LIES nine miles to the east of Carrbank, a pleasant and comparatively unspoilt village on the north-western bank of the Brent, a slow-flowing and navigable river which winds its way through four counties before emptying its waters in the Humber. To reach it, Crompton had to pass through Netherlea, a hamlet well known to tourists for its thatched-roof cottages and the triangular green on which stood the original quintain post from which the one inn took its name. Outside the inn stood a giant chestnut, around which had been built an octagonal seat. It was here that Crompton drew in, and invited Lisbeth Ann to "hop off".

"You're not going drinking, Johnny!" she pouted as she tried to pat her wind-swept hair into some semblance of order.

Crompton gently pulled her hands down from her head. "Don't alter it, Lisbeth Ann. It looks nice like that!"

She blinked her surprise. "*You* think I look nice, Johnny. I didn't think you ever looked at me!"

Crompton grinned sheepishly. "Perhaps I haven't until now. Lord, isn't it grand to get out of town, and away from the traffic, and the rush of the office, and the smells of industry. Somehow, you know, you don't look the same in town. Strikes me I've been going around like a blind man. Things aren't the same here. . . ."

"You'll have to get out into the country more often," she said softly. "It's lovely in these villages, and when you get down by the river, at Littleby Ferry, and Willowford. . . ."

"Yes, we must," said Crompton. "You'd come with me, Lisbeth Ann?"

"Oh yes!" she said a trifle too enthusiastically. "I'd love it—with you."

Crompton grimaced. "I'm afraid I'm not very good company at present. Still, let's make the most of the break before we go on to Rainley. Come on."

He took her hand and began to lead her to the inn.

"Johnny! You aren't going drinking!"

He glanced round at her anxious face, and shook his head. "I haven't finished drinking, but I have finished boozing. We're going to the coffee room now."

"I'm glad, Johnny."

"I don't know why I'm talking like this," said Crompton. "Perhaps it's because I so seldom have anyone to talk to in town—only the boys in the Falcon, and the old dear at the digs, and she only talks about money, and her dear husband who died of a heart attack five years ago after giving her a beating up. No, it's occurred to me within the past few hours that I've been something of a clot."

There seemed to be little that Lisbeth Ann could say in reply, and so she asked: "Why are we going to Rainley, Johnny?"

He did not answer, but led the way through the passage of the inn to the coffee room at the rear, the windows of which overlooked a well-cared-for flower garden.

He ordered coffee and biscuits from the innkeeper's wife, and handed the bowl of demerara sugar to Lisbeth Ann.

"I'm going to see Uncle John's mistress," he said in a low voice.

"Frances!"

Crompton looked up. "You know about her?"

"I actually know her, Johnny. She's a nice person."

"Well, blow me down," exclaimed Crompton. "Here am I trying to shield you from knowledge of the wicked world, and you know more about it than I do!"

"He was going to marry her, you know!"

"Oh," said Crompton.

"And she wasn't his mistress, either! He'd had several, but Frances was not one of them. She's a good, kind person. Her husband was the schoolmaster at Rainley. He died six or seven years ago. I'll tell you something else if you'll promise not to tell anyone else—"

Crompton stretched across the table and pressed her hand. "Half a minute, before we indulge in confidences, Lisbeth Ann. You realise that I'm Bowden's chief suspect for your uncle's murder?"

"Well, I didn't know, but I suspected it. You aren't, of course!"

"I'm not," said Crompton, "but here is the point. I have to clear myself, and I don't want you to tell me anything in confidence which I might feel tempted to use in the process of clearing myself."

Lisbeth Ann smiled at him. "I was going to tell you about Uncle John's will—and you will learn about that from the solicitors sooner or later."

"That's true," Crompton agreed.

"I don't get anything from it."

"You don't? Then who does?"

"Charlie Carrington and Frances."

"Charlie Carrington!"

She nodded solemnly.

"And Frances Mundeham!"

"After Uncle John had the bust-up with Charlie he raved round the house like a madman when he got home. He was going to make a new will, give the lot to Frances, and she and I would have the *News* when he died—I get Mother's share, of course, and Dad's interest in the radio company."

"Yes, that's right," murmured Crompton. "Does Charlie know he's among the winners?"

"Yes. You see, Uncle John thought it out. He knew Frances is a good business woman, but that wasn't enough. He wanted someone who knew something about writing as well. He reckoned it would make a well-balanced team. After all, Charlie's done about everything possible in the writing game . . ."

"That's true," said Crompton. After a moment he looked her straight in the eyes and asked: "Did Charlie know he was likely to change his will?"

She stared back. "Oh no, Johnny! Not that! You don't think Charlie would—would do *that*!"

"Somebody did," Crompton replied, "and I've no personal wish to finish up at Brankley!"

There was another long silence, and then Lisbeth Ann said: "Johnny, you're investigating Uncle John's death off your own bat, aren't you?"

"I've got to do that, surely!"

Lisbeth Ann shook her head. "No, you haven't, Johnny. I'd like to help you. I can, you know!"

Crompton regarded her slowly, and then a smile crept to his lips. "Odd, isn't it? For all these months I've just regarded you as a reporter, a cog in a machine, a shorthand note-taker, and niece of the boss."

"You'll let me help you, Johnny?" she pleaded.

"What the heck can you do to help?" he asked.

"Keep my eyes and ears open."

Crompton came to a sudden decision, and nodded. "Okay, Lisbeth Ann! It's a deal!" He added: "God knows how I shall manage to repay you!"

"Perhaps He'll work that out as well," she replied softly.

Crompton rang the bell. "We'll have more coffee, please," he said when it was answered. "Is Davidson making himself a nuisance?" he asked when they were served.

"He's a nasty piece of work," said Lisbeth Ann. "You know what he's after, don't you?"

"I don't like to say it," replied Crompton.

"You're not quite right, Johnny. Davidson wants to marry me so that he can run the paper."

"He—what!" almost bawled Crompton.

"That's it," she nodded. "He's tried nearly all his techniques up to now—I'm not so innocent as you might think. I have been around."

"It's only a few months since you were in school," said Crompton.

"Times are faster," she said. "Davidson has tried everything from buying me chocolates to tearing my clothes from my back."

"Seymour said he suspected something like that had been happening. I'll break his blasted neck when I get back."

She pressed his hand, which was still holding her own. "Davidson is my affair, Johnny. I can manage him! You've more important things to do."

She glanced at the grandfather clock in the corner of the room. "It's turned twelve, Johnny. Think we ought to be going?"

"Turned twelve, eh? It's Friday, and technically our half-day off. What say we have lunch?"

Her eyes shone. "Together?"

Crompton laughed aloud. "I'm going to look damn silly eating it alone under the chestnut tree."

Lisbeth Ann smiled at him. "That's the first time I've heard you give a laugh that wasn't a dirty one!"

"Must be the fresh air and change of scenery," he said.

"Yes, Johnny," she said. "Perhaps that's it!"

After lunch they went on to see Frances Mundeham, and Crompton took Lisbeth Ann to the cottage with him. If she knew the woman so well there was little point in her spending an hour feeding already over-fed swans on the river.

He looked round the tidy and well-kept cottage, and at the bright-eyed and neat little woman who had welcomed them at her porched door. He shook his head. Davidson was a liar and a cad. There was nothing wrong with the morals of this lady.

She embraced Lisbeth Ann and kissed her cheek. "I'm so glad you came. I was hoping you'd find time, dear. And I'm glad you brought your friend along." Lisbeth Ann giggled. "I didn't, Frances. He brought me, with the idea of letting me feed the swans while he had a talk with Uncle John's mistress!"

"Lisbeth Ann!" exclaimed Crompton.

Frances Mundeham gave a wry smile. "I'm used to that slur by now—although I assure you there's no truth in it. I could have been that, you know, but if I did little else for him I believe I showed him that there are other kinds of women in the world. Anyway, dear, you haven't introduced us yet."

Lisbeth Ann appeared to have a knack, unfortunate in Crompton's opinion, of going too directly to the point.

"This is Johnny Crompton, Frances. He's chief reporter on the paper, and one of the police suspects for causing Uncle John's death."

"Oh, goodness, Lisbeth Ann!" protested Crompton.

Frances Mundeham stood in front of him and looked up into his face for a full minute. She shook her head. "No, Johnny Crompton, you didn't kill Edward Packman!"

"Well, thank God somebody believes that!" said Crompton.

"But I do, Johnny!" said Lisbeth Ann.

"You know," said Frances Mundeham, "I think we three should stick together. The Bible says that a three-fold cord is not easily broken. I like you, Johnny Crompton."

"Compliments are not much in my line," Crompton said hesitantly, "but I'd like to return that one."

Frances suddenly became efficient. "You two dears had anything to eat lately?"

"We lunched at the Quintain," said Lisbeth Ann.

"Then a cup of tea? You can always drink a cup of tea. Then you can—er—interview Edward's mistress, Johnny!"

"Oh, don't rub that in," said Crompton. "It was what Davidson told me. I'd never even heard of you."

"Davidson? Harry Davidson, you mean?"

"Why, yes—"

Her lips went tight. "We'll talk about Harry Davidson over a cup of tea. Lisbeth Ann, find some magazines for Johnny, and then come and help me. I'll put the kettle on."

She bustled away, and Lisbeth Ann began rummaging under the cushions.

"You've been here before?" asked Crompton.

"Oh yes, often! Uncle John wanted me to get to know Frances before he married her. We should live together, you see! I was to learn to drive the car, and we were moving in here. I was to drive Uncle John to work every day."

"Look," said Crompton; "what was he really like at home? I'm thinking about Omar Khayyam. . . ."

"When anything upset him he had the vilest temper of anyone I've ever known, Johnny, but when things were going well—as they generally were—he was very nice indeed. Frances could handle him, of course!"

"I can well believe that," grinned Crompton. "I think she could handle anybody or anything! A most capable woman."

"Lisbeth Ann!" Frances called from the kitchen.

"You'd better go," said Crompton.

"She probably wants to pump me about you."

"I'd thought that one out."

Lisbeth Ann paused in the doorway. "I won't be long, Johnny!"

Crompton smoothed a hand over his face when he was alone. Somehow, in a way he could not define, his life seemed to have taken a new turn in the past few hours, in the past very few hours in fact. From a world of haste, hurry and intense competition he had stepped into a softer, slower, more equable one. He sank back into a chintz-covered chair, gave up his body to its embracing resilience, and decided that he liked it. He was beginning to understand Packman a little better now, and yet was puzzled by the two-sidedness of the man—a man who could be a copy-demanding tyrant for eight or nine hours a day, and then fit himself into the peaceful comfort of a home like this.

The two women arrived with the tea trolley, and Frances poured tea.

"You like my little home?" she asked.

"So much that I don't want to go back to town," said Crompton. "I'd like a place like this. It revives old ambitions."

"You'd like to write, of course," Frances said as she handed him a cup of tea.

"How did you guess?"

"Oh, call it a woman's intuition if you like," she replied. "You're far too sensitive for the rough and tumble of a newspaper office. Mind you, it isn't all intuition! Edward used to talk about his staff!"

"I'm glad I never overheard him!" said Crompton.

She leaned towards him. "What would you like to write, Johnny?"

"Novels—good novels, I hope. About people doing things, people really living. About people breaking free from—yes, from civilisation. People living in homes like yours. People who are not concerned with *getting* so much as with *being*. There are real people in the world, and those are the people I'd like to write about."

"You must do that," said Frances. "We must see that you have a chance to do that."

"You must do that, Johnny! You must write!" said Lisbeth Ann.

Crompton finished his tea, and put the cup and saucer on the trolley.

"Those few minutes were a nice dream, Mrs. Mundeham!"

"Frances!" she corrected. She smiled at him. "I quite understand. You came here to interview me. What do you wish to know, Mr. Crompton?"

"Come off it, Frances!" protested Lisbeth Ann.

Frances patted her hand. "We are faced with a very intense reporter who has a noose hanging over his head, dear. Now, Johnny, you wanted to know about Davidson?"

"I think it might help—and it might not. I don't know what's important and what isn't at the moment."

"We must use the scientific method," said Frances. "Collect all the available facts, and from them form a hypothesis, and later a theory, and then seek to prove the theory."

"That sounds hard-boiled!" said Crompton.

Frances smiled almost too sweetly. "I was once a science mistress in a large school in the south of England—long before I became mistress to an editor. However, Harry Davidson is a nasty piece of work. He's a riverside pub crawler, and he saw Edward and myself, together on several occasions, and tried to blackmail him. He thought we were ashamed of our friendship because we went to quiet inns, and foolishly assumed that Edward would pay up sooner than be—er—exposed."

"And he didn't pay up!"

"He didn't pay up, and he was going to sack Davidson at the end of the month."

"This is new to me, and interesting," said Crompton. "I'm beginning to see daylight at the end of the tunnel."

"And the next you wish to ask?"

"Did you wait for Edward John in St. Gudulph's Gate on Thursday evening?"

"I've never waited for Edward in St. Gudulph's Gate nor anywhere else in Carrbank!" she replied firmly.

"Davidson said you did—at the end of St. Gudulph's Court!"

"Davidson is a liar."

"I'm beginning to see that for myself."

"And the next question, Johnny?"

"The widow at the Ferryman, below Thorpe Bridge."

"What about her?"

"Had Edward John any interest in her?"

Frances shook her head, and her lips compressed into a straight line. "It was Mrs. Cartwright who was interested in Edward, to the point of embarrassment. She used to join us at a table, and in the end we ceased going there."

She arched her pencilled eyebrows. "Davidson information again?"

Crompton nodded. "Another question, please. I'm aware it's nosing into your private affairs, but if you didn't meet him in Carrbank, how did you meet?"

"Well, he was also uncertain as to the time he would get away from the office, and he used to come out by taxi, and I'd run him back later in my little coupe, or run him to a bus stop and he would finish the journey by bus. We were trying to be discreet, although actually there was no reason why we should have been. If the truth is told Edward was a little afraid of being thought of as a bachelor gay who had left love late, and then fallen hard. All men are boys, you know, and Edward was very self-conscious."

"The more I hear of the man the more I'm surprised," said Crompton.

"Men are so often surprised at the obvious," Frances remarked. "How many men, for instance, are aware of the fact that they are falling in love when they are actually head over heels?"

"Oh well, no man but a clot could miss that fact!" said Crompton. "You see the girl, you like her, you fall in love, and start chasing her—deliberately!"

"Now fancy that!" said Frances. "Our Johnny Crompton can see where he is going, Lisbeth Ann!" Lisbeth Ann did not reply, but a queer little smile played round her mouth.

"Johnny is far too busy to fall in love," said Frances. "He has to save his neck from the noose, keep the paper going, and find a way of achieving his writing ambitions. Johnny will never have time to see a girl and chase her—deliberately."

"I think you're laughing at me," protested Crompton. "I don't know why, but you are."

"Do you think I would be so unkind?" said Frances. "Anyway, is there anything else I can tell you?"

"You seem very composed."

"You mean considering I have lost Edward?"

"Er—yes. I shouldn't have said that."

"In some ways you are very unsophisticated," she replied. "You don't expect a woman to wear her heart on her sleeve, and do her weeping in public, do you? I've very little to look forward to now, Johnny Crompton, but I've met tragedy before and I know how to treat him. It's no good running away to hide. You have to get in close and face him, and then outface him. Otherwise you're lost. You should remember that when you start writing your novels."

Crompton looked at Lisbeth Ann. "I think we should go now, don't you? I ought to see the solicitors, or the accountants, or somebody, and find out what is going to happen to the paper."

Frances nodded. "You should do that. Unless Edward altered his will in the last week I shall be a partner in the firm, and on that premise I shall ask you to stay on for a time until we can work out a somewhat gentler policy than Edward favoured. After that, you must write. . . ."

The goodbyes were said, and with Lisbeth Ann perched behind him Crompton drove from the village. He took a roundabout route home so that he could look at the various inns at which Davidson said Packman and Frances had spent their leisure hours.

Half a mile below the Ferryman Inn he drove from the road to the tow-path, and stopped the engine.

"Something wrong, Johnny?" asked Lisbeth Ann.

"Nothing, absolutely nothing," Crompton replied. "I just want to soak in a bit more of this country peace before going back to town and into battle once more. Let's walk down the path for a few minutes."

Lisbeth Ann walked demurely by his side beneath the willows and aspens. Eventually he stopped against a five-barred gate that led into lush water meadows, and they watched the water birds playing up-tails-all as they looked for food.

Johnny turned to say something to her, and then looked into her eyes. The next moment he swept her into his arms and kissed her full on the lips. Then he released her, stared wonderingly, and said: "Now why did I do that?"

"I—I don't know, Johnny," she replied softly.

Her eyes were shining, and she stood without movement, smiling at him. "I don't know, Johnny," she repeated.

He grabbed her hand. "Come on. Let's get back to town."

As Lisbeth Ann fixed her skirt round her knees and tucked it against the sides of the rear saddle, Crompton said in a matter-of-fact voice: "Frances is something of a wise woman, isn't she?"

"You don't know how wise she is!" said Lisbeth Ann.

8
ACCOUNTING FOR MANY THINGS

THERE HAD BEEN happenings in town while they had been in the country, as Crompton soon discovered when he went into the reporters' room where Seymour was writing up the committal proceedings.

"Good job you're back," he said. "Both Bowden and Crossley have been after you. Charlie's been here in a sweat, and Lisbeth Ann's housekeeper came raving in, weeping all over the place about poor, dear Master John, and the way Lisbeth Ann had neglected her. She seemed to be under the impression that she was spending last night with you in some sinful rampage or other. I asks you!"

"I stayed with the Carringtons," Lisbeth Ann said indignantly, "and Cora Carrington rang to say I was staying. The very idea of staying with Johnny all night!"

Seymour turned from his machine, his face completely dead pan. "Shocking to suggest that you would even consider doing anything like that! Much sooner have a night with me, wouldn't you, dear?"

Lisbeth Ann swiped at him, and Crompton caught her arm before it landed on his ear.

"Cut it out, the pair of you. Look, Seymour, my lad, any idea why the coppers wanted to see me?"

Seymour's grin faded. "I don't want to tell tales, and I don't want to put ideas into your head, but I do know that Davidson went round to Bowden's office this morning. I nipped out of court for a smoke, and spotted his back going into the C.I.D. room. His front had already gone in."

"Hm!" said Crompton. "Know anything else?"

"Well now," said Seymour, "you know me, and you know that eavesdropping is the last thing I'd do in any circumstances!"

"Go on with it," said Crompton grimly.

"Purely by accident I wandered down that end of the corridor, towards Bowden's door. It was closed, but I happened to drop my fag just as my shoelace came undone, and so I had my ear near the keyhole for a few seconds. I heard your name twice, uttered by Bowden's voice, and heard it three times in Davidson's voice. To use police parlance, I should say that Harry boy was laying an information against you."

"Nice of him!" commented Crompton.

"After court I learned from Morgan and Newnes that Bowden, Crossley, and a sergeant from Burnham gave 'em all a good grilling this morning, and seemed interested in the possibility of Charlie having moved from the Falcon on Thursday night. They remembered him going out to the toilet twice, and that on one occasion you accompanied him, and on the second, while you were out, he was missing for some time. Charlie says he met some fellow or other in the vestibule and was talking to him. He doesn't know who the man was, and could only say that it was some fan who wanted his autograph for his little boy. At the moment, everybody appears to be under suspicion for something or other. Except me, and my spotless reputation saves me from molestation by the police."

"If they ever find out what you are like you'll spend the rest of your life in quod!" said Crompton. "Looks as if things are warming up!"

"Shouldn't have been such a clot as to admit that you found him!" said Seymour.

"For once you have something, Bill," replied Crompton. "That was a stupid thing to do."

"Honesty is a mug's game," commented Seymour. "I'm not owning up to anything I know!"

"Do you know anything?"

Seymour registered mock indignation. "Me? Know anything? I know the whole blooming lot."

"You know sweet Fanny Adams!" said Crompton.

"Those who live longest see most," replied Seymour, "and I don't intend having a knife in my back, thank you."

"That's a laudable ambition," said Crompton, "but there's nothing to stop me shoving your head through the window!"

"I—I was kidding, Johnny. You know how it is with this blooming job round you! If you didn't joke you'd do a bunk, or bust into tears or something. E.J. was a bit of a so-and-so at times, but he was—well, he was decent to me taking him all round. You know!"

Crompton patted him on the back. "I know just how you feel, Bill, and in this ruddy profession you can't afford to have feelings."

He happened to meet Lisbeth Ann's eyes as he spoke. He was aware of a flush of blood rising to his cheeks, and lamely he added: "Or can you?"

Brusquely he asked for the first folios of the committal copy, and went to his room to sub it. Lisbeth Ann stayed with Seymour.

It was with something like self-disgust that he discovered a telephone message from Baxby written on his pad. He was so concerned with his own predicament that he had completely forgotten Danny Moss. The message assured him that Danny was hanged at nine o'clock without hitch.

"At any rate, boy," Crompton said aloud, "you went out without Packman's black banner hailing you!"

He spiked the note and got down to the subbing, and later to consideration of the diary of events for the coming week. That done, he rang Packman's solicitors and asked for some indication of the paper's possible future. He was told that there was no secret about Packman's will. His estate was to be shared between Mrs. Frances Mundeham and Mr. Charles Carrington. There were, however, such matters as probate involved, and until probate had been granted the accountants would act as trustees and administrators of the paper in full consultation with themselves, the solicitors, as executors.

So Crompton rang the accountants, and was asked to call round to see them. He went straight away, and came from their office with instructions to act as editor for the time being, and to make no changes in policy or make-up unless expressly ordered to do so.

This news he passed to Lisbeth Ann, adding that there seemed to be no reason why they should not tame down Packman's policy, and perhaps make more friends in the town. "We might also push the circulation up by a few hundreds," he added. "Your position is the oddest of the lot. You are virtually boss, with a half-share—when you get it. You work for yourself, and if you want time off you have to ask me for it, and I have to ask you before I can grant it!"

"Your sense of humour's coming to life, Johnny!" Lisbeth Ann enthused.

"And a darn funny time for it to do it!" he replied. Changing both mood and subject, he asked:—"Get anything out of Bill? Does he know anything, or was he just kidding?"

Lisbeth Ann was slow to reply. "I think he knows something. I don't know what it is, or who it concerns, but one thing's certain—he is scared stiff of Harry Davidson."

"It may mean nothing," said Crompton. "Davidson seems to have had a yen for power, and if he couldn't get any change from Uncle John and Frances he probably took it out of the kid! I must have been blind not to see the things that were happening round me in this office."

"Uncle John kept you hard at it most of the time, Johnny. You should be able to ease off a wee bit now."

"What? With your uncle gone, Davidson acting awkward, and me having to combine an acting editorship with reporting? We haven't enough staff for any slacking, my girl."

"Pull Charlie in!" Lisbeth Ann suggested. "He's just finished the new novel, and you know he always loafs round for a few weeks before starting a new one—y'know, while he's thinking out the next."

"Could do that," said Crompton. "I don't think I'd have to ask gracious permission of the accountants, either. Edward John used to pull him in during busy periods, and so it would conform with routine."

"Johnny," said Lisbeth Ann; "have they been laying down the law to you?"

Crompton gave a wry smile. "From one thing and another they probably realise that I might feel tempted to make a few changes. I received very strict instructions not to start mucking about with the paper."

Lisbeth Ann was silent for a few moments, and then she asked: "What are you going to do with yourself for the rest of the day? There are no jobs on the diary, no more writing-up to be done, and—and you've stopped drinking!"

Crompton smiled. "You've stuck me with a poser! What the deuce does a reporter do if he isn't working or boozing? I've no hobbies, no garden to dig, and—"

"Sweet Fanny Adams?" suggested Lisbeth Ann.

Crompton nodded. "That's about the size of it. On the other hand I wouldn't be surprised if Bowden and Crossley find me some writing to do—and that's quite a bright idea! I'll go round to the warehouse and offer to write up my statement for them."

"Er—can I come?"

"Whaffor?" asked Crompton.

"Well, I'm determined I'm not going back to be wept over by Mrs. Barrowcliffe. . . ."

"You've got to live somewhere!"

"But not with Mrs. Barrowcliffe! How would you like to spend your spare time hearing all about the pranks that Master John got up to when he was a boy? And it'll be even worse now he's gone."

"You've still got to live somewhere!"

"Cora Carrington will have me—willingly."

"You've still got to pay board and lodging!"

"Suppose I go to live with Frances?"

"The same applies."

"With differences."

"Such as?"

"Cora has Charlie, and Frances has nobody. She has a little money, and she could grub-stake me until the will is settled, and then I could pay her back in a lump sum."

"It's nine miles from the office."

"I've got some money, Johnny. You could advise me about buying a scooter, and I could get to town and back without any difficulty."

Crompton regarded her slowly. She had her heels dug in.

"What about his house and furniture?" he asked.

"If his estate is being shared between Charlie and Frances it means, surely, that it will all have to be sold, and the proceeds shared."

"You seem to have thought out the whole thing!"

"Well, somebody had to do my thinking for me, and I'd nobody else!" she said pointedly.

Crompton sniffed. "I'll help you as much as I can, Lisbeth Ann. Looks to me as if we'll have to stick together for a time, doesn't it?"

"Does it?" she asked, almost coldly.

"Well, I mean," Crompton said uncomfortably, "you'll need help from me at first in running the paper, and during that time I'll need your backing—not that I expect either Charlie or Frances to cut up rough. They're both human types."

Lisbeth Ann pushed her hair back from her face. "Business can be quite a business, can't it? And here's another one, Johnny! What if I decide to sell my share, and pull out? I'm not too fond of journalism, you know! I can think of many other things, much more interesting, I could do with the money."

"Such as?" Crompton asked curiously.

"A girl is allowed to keep some secrets," she reminded him.

"Sorry," he said. "I wasn't trying to pry. Anyway, I'd better get off to the warehouse and see Bowden's secretarial staff."

"I'll come with you," said Lisbeth Ann firmly. "I know you! You'll put your neck in the noose if you aren't watched. And when we come away you can show me what kind of scooter to buy."

"One thing does occur to me," Crompton said slowly. "Wouldn't it be wise to ask Frances if you can go to her?"

Lisbeth Ann gave an enigmatical smile. "We fixed all that up while we were making tea!"

"Oh, my lord," said Crompton. "Women!"

Crompton was never quite sure how it happened, but he dictated a statement at the police station, had it read back to him, and signed it, and then he found himself signing a form as witness for Lisbeth Ann, who was buying a scooter. Still later he found himself taking her to tea in the cinema café, then into the cinema to see the programme, and at last, at half-past eight, he was standing with her outside the cinema.

"What now?" he asked the air, aloud.

"I've had a lovely day, thank you," said Lisbeth Ann demurely. "I'd better get to the bus station and see what time there's a bus for Rainley."

Crompton stared uncomprehendingly at her. "You've had a lovely day," he said in a flat monotone. "Your uncle was murdered last night. You've had to identify him at the mortuary. You've been grilled by the C.I.D. You've left him and gone to live with a friend. You have to catch a bus and ride nine miles to the lane-end, and then walk quarter of a mile through a dark lane to your new home. And—you've—had—a—lovely—day!"

"The nice things have outbalanced the nasty ones," she said.

"What nice things?"

She shrugged. "You're a man, Johnny. You wouldn't understand!"

Johnny Crompton was beginning to feel tired, but an idea slowly filtered through the consciousness. He could not leave her to go to Rainley alone. . . .

"We'll go back to the office and get the scooter out," he said. "I'll run you to Rainley."

"Oh, Johnny! Would you do that?"

As they walked down St. Gudulph's Gate he was aware that she was linking her arm through his.

Half an hour later he was sipping coffee before a log fire with Frances Mundeham and Lisbeth Ann.

"Did you remember to collect your pay packet?" asked Lisbeth Ann.

Crompton laughed. "Never entered my head. Why?"

"Well, I forgot to tell you. Harry Davidson left an envelope for you in the general office. He apparently changed his mind about not writing up the cage birds, and he had slung the envelope in and walked out without a word to anybody."

"We'll see it in the morning," said Crompton. "Forget copy for tonight. It'll come in useful, nevertheless. Thing that's puzzling me is what the heck we can do, and can't do, with your uncle's story. I can't remember hearing of any paper that ever had this one to work out."

He yawned heavily, and apologised. "This fire," he said, "and the fact that I haven't been to bed for forty-eight hours. Forty-eight hours! Lord, I hadn't realised it."

"And I've been trailing you round buying a scooter, and taking me to tea, and to the pictures . . . !"

"We went together," said Crompton. "I don't take girls to the pictures! Allies standing four-square before a common foe and all that!"

Frances seemed to be amused by the suggestion, and made no secret of her smile.

"What's funny?" Crompton asked.

"You," Frances said bluntly. "You hate admitting that you have any feelings."

"Any minute now I must be getting back to town," said Crompton. "I'm almost dropping asleep—and that's bad manners."

Frances got up and went to the far side of the long dim-lighted lounge. As she returned, the first bars of a Chopin nocturne entered the room from the radiogram.

"Oh, for a home like this!" sighed Crompton.

The music eventually ended and was replaced by other nocturnes. He lolled deeper in his chair, and slid easily into deep sleep.

Lisbeth Ann watched him closely. "He's sound asleep!" she whispered.

"He should be," Frances said with an amused smile. She crossed the hearth, loosened his tie, and unbuttoned his shirt neck. Then she bent down and unfastened his shoes and slipped them from his feet.

"You'll wake him!" said Lisbeth Ann.

Frances shook her head. "He was far too tired to ride that thing home, dear. He might have come to grief. He can stay here all night, have breakfast with us, and you can go into town together in the morning."

Lisbeth Ann gasped. "You've—you've doped him, Frances!"

"Something like that, dear," she admitted. "You see, he's had a tough time—and it isn't over for him yet by long chalks. What rest would he get in a stuffy bedroom in digs?"

She took Johnny's legs and swung them round on the settee. "There, my lad, you can sleep the sleep of the innocent!"

She glanced at Lisbeth Ann as she walked to the doorway and switched off the light. "You can kiss him good-night if you wish, dear. Even a tough guy like Johnny Crompton can't resist when he's doped!"

"Frances! Don't be a beast!" Lisbeth Ann protested.

"And close the lounge door behind you when you come out! I'll be in the sitting room!"

A minute later Lisbeth Ann, somewhat flushed, gently closed the door and joined Frances.

"What about the scooter?" she asked.

"In the garage and locked up, dear. I pushed it round an hour ago!"

Lisbeth Ann put her arms round Frances's waist and hugged her. "You're wonderful!"

"My husband Sam used to say that I was descended from Machiavelli—but then he was prejudiced. All husbands are, as you'll find out for yourself."

She suddenly broke off. "There's someone pulling up in a car."

She pushed Lisbeth Ann's arms away, and hurried across the room to peep round the edge of the curtain.

"Vanish to your room," she said.

"My room?"

"And stay there. The police are outside, and I wouldn't be surprised if they are looking for me."

"But why you?" asked Lisbeth Ann.

"Harry Davidson always said he would get square with both of us."

The front gate squeaked on its hinges.

"On second thoughts," said Frances, "go into the lounge with Johnny. You can sit in the firelight, and will not have to switch on the light. Stay there, *no matter what happens*! Now go, child!"

There came a heavy thudding at the front door.

9
DISCUSSION AT TOP LEVEL

NEITHER LISBETH ANN nor Crompton learned anything from Frances of her interview with Crossley, except that Crossley came alone and was regarded as a gentleman of a very high order. The interview lasted an hour and a half, and when Crossley left Frances had to wake Lisbeth Ann, who had gone to sleep on the hearth with her head resting on Crompton's settee. Crompton was still dead to the world, and was most apologetic when Frances roused him next morning with a cup of tea. He was not told that his long sleep had been assisted from the medicine chest, and he apologised again and again for his discourtesy in falling asleep.

"Must have been dog tired," he said. "I feel very scruffy, too. Think I could have a wash?"

"A shave as well if you can use my husband's cut-throat razor. I'll show you the bathroom, and give you twenty minutes before breakfast is served."

It was a much-refreshed Crompton who drove back to town an hour and a quarter later with Lisbeth Ann. They went straight to the office, and before going to his room Crompton called in the general office and took over his pay packet and the envelope left for him by Davidson.

"Isn't it copy?" Lisbeth Ann asked as Crompton ran his finger under the flap and took out a single sheet of notepaper.

"It is not," Crompton said slowly as he read the note. "Here, read it for yourself. Davidson has left. He doesn't fancy working for a dirty murderer, the mistress of the late boss, the teenage niece of the late boss, and a churner-out of crime novels."

"Why, the rat!" Lisbeth Ann exploded. "Gone to Manchester after a job, and will send his address to the police when he gets one."

Crompton strode through to the reporters' room, and back again. "He hasn't left his copy. I'll have to ring Tranter, the secretary, and ask him if he'll lend me the record book to work from."

He thumbed the directory, and then dialled the number of the Cage Bird Society secretary.

"You'll realise the difficulties we are up against," he explained, "and our reporter has gone away without leaving his report of your show. I was wondering—eh?"

Lisbeth Ann nodded her head wisely. "He never went!"

Crompton listened as the secretary told him what he thought about being let down by the non-attendance of a representative of the *Borough News*. It was the first time in the history of the society that they had been ignored in this way, and his committee were—

Crompton cut into the diatribe, and after three or four minutes of heavily applying a reporter's best flannel he calmed down Tranter and was assured of the utmost cooperation in preparing a report of the show. The secretary casually sympathised for the death of the editor.

Replacing the handset, Crompton ran a hand round the inside of his collar. "So that's that! The next thing is to work out how he did it."

"You really think it was Davidson, Johnny?"

"I've been suspicious since yesterday."

"But why?"

Crompton nodded. "That's what's got me. It just doesn't make sense nor reason. You might hit a bloke because you don't like him, or because you row with him—as I did, but you don't stick a knife in him. A hot-tempered type like myself might do so, but Davy was the cool and calculating type. Anyway, ignoring the motive, how could he have done it?"

"He'd lost his key!"

"He said!"

"But then why borrow mine on Wednesday night?"

"To make it look as if he really had lost it. See?"

"I see," said Lisbeth Ann. "In that case he could let himself in when he wanted."

"But," Crompton said slowly, "he didn't go out the same way, or he would have been seen by Mornington or Bowden—and I'm certain there was someone up here when I was finding your uncle downstairs. Probably hiding behind the toilet door, which was part open. From there he could see and not be seen. Now I wonder. . . ."

He walked to the corridor and stared at the casement window that overlooked the gabled bays of the printing works. He uncatched it, pushed open the window, and looked out.

"My name isn't Crossley," he said softly, "but if those aren't footmarks on the blue slates I'm a Dutchman. Hold everything! I'm going out on the roof."

"Be careful, Johnny! Don't break your neck!"

"That," Crompton replied drily, "is exactly what I am trying to avoid!"

He drew himself up to the sill, sat down, and lowered himself to the leaded gully four feet below. He dropped on all fours and began to climb up the slates. Reaching the ridge he saw that he had the large north-light panes to avoid, and that meant making his way along the ridge to the side of the building. Then he began the climb up the second slope. He paused as he heard a peculiar scratching and scraping on the other side of it. He drew himself up cautiously, and looked straight into the huge face and smiling eyes of Murray Bowden. Bowden smiled, and said "Boo!"

Crompton returned the smile, heaved himself to the ridge to sit astride it, and offered his cigarette case.

"Don't mind if I do," said Bowden. "Have a light. Comfortable? Then perhaps we can compare notes?"

"It's easy from my side of it," said Crompton. "What's the drop like into the field at the back?"

"An athletic type like you could manage it quite nicely. I've left Dobson down there cursing me—I had to stand on his back to get my fingers on the edge of the gulley. The drop into the field is about eight feet."

He blew a whiff of smoke down his nose. "Any news for me?"

"Davidson has pulled out on us."

Crompton took the note from his pocket and handed it to Bowden, who read it and handed it back. "Hang on to that, please. On second thoughts I'll take it now. We can't have potential witnesses running loose like this. Davidson might be important."

"He tried to shop me, didn't he?" asked Crompton.

Bowden looked round. "Quite a view from up here, really. I've often wondered why they left that field at the back."

"Belongs to the firm," said Crompton. "It was for planned expansion some day or other. Still, I asked you a question. Davidson tried to shop me?"

Bowden gave a grim smile. "Brother, if we believed everything we were told you'd be inside now on a variety of charges. Harry boy did not appear to like you, nor Packman, nor Mrs. Mundeham."

"Who is a born lady," said Crompton.

Bowden inclined his head in a light bow. "With which we all agree. That is where Davidson boobed. If he had only gone for you, or for you and Packman, we might have listened a little harder, but when he included the lady we only bent a dubious ear."

He puffed at his cigarette for a minute. "This is probably the first time for months that we have been agreeable with each other, Johnny!"

"It's the altitude," said Crompton. "More oxygen and such things up here to purify our bodies and our minds."

"Where's the girl?" asked Bowden.

Crompton jerked a thumb. "Back there waiting for the results of the expedition."

"How are you doing with her?"

"I'm not doing anything with her!"

Bowden snorted. "You should be. She's a nice girl, and needs someone to look after her."

"Why pick me when you and Crossley have inner visions of me wearing a rope round my neck."

"You're not a bad reporter," said Bowden, sadly shaking his head, "but in all other worldly affairs you are as dim as rushlight! Think there might be a cup of tea back in your camp?"

"It can be arranged."

"Then let's trek that way, shall we? You lead the way, Mr. Hillary."

As Crompton lowered himself down the slope he asked: "How did you get the idea about this as a possible exit?"

"Possible entrance," Bowden corrected him. "The latch was up, for one thing. We spotted it on Thursday night. Then there was the matter of the lost key—see what I mean?"

"For once two great minds have run on parallel lines."

"If you start comparing mine with yours I'll do you for defamation of character! Blimey, I could do with a rope and an ice-axe," grunted Bowden.

He hauled himself to the ridge of the second bay, and paused there to raise his trilby to Lisbeth Ann, still waiting at the window. "I always call round by this route on Saturdays," he said. "Can you organise a pot of tea for three?"

Lisbeth Ann nodded, and vanished.

When they reached Crompton's room and had dusted down each other's backs and backsides with Crompton's private clothes-brush, Crompton asked: "Look, chum. Answer me one question, will you? Do you know who did the job?"

"I think so," said Bowden. "That's as far as I'm going with you, for while I can say unofficially that you are in the clear I can't forget that you promised to make a monkey of me! Tell you what I'll do—if you get there before I do, I'll put a fiver in the benevolent fund."

"Police or journalists?"

"Police, of course! You don't think I'd do anything to make the life of a reporter any easier, do you?"

"You never have done up to now," replied Crompton sadly, "and at your time of life it's getting a bit late to start."

"Why, you—"

Crompton sat astride a chair and stared at the inspector. "Davidson didn't do the job he was supposed to do on Thursday night. He never went near the bird show!"

"I know," said Bowden. "If you want a bit more information I can tell you that Bill Seymour didn't sit through *Thunder Rock* beyond the first act, and he and Davidson met in the bar of the Oak Tree in Cannon Street. They were together for ten minutes round about eight o'clock time, and we can't trace the movements of either after that time. I'm only telling you this in case you can find a way of filling the gap for us."

"But Seymour wrote his review of the play."

"Invented it then," said Bowden. "He only saw the first act, and came out just as the lights went down for the second. Has he seen the play before?"

"Not as a reporter. No!"

"Davidson?"

Crompton went to the bookshelves behind the door, and returned with a double handful of programmes and show schedules. "Take half," he said, thrusting a pile into Bowden's great hands.

It was Bowden who announced success three minutes later. "*Thunder Rock*, presented by the Albion Players at the Maddox Hall on three successive nights last December—from the fourth to the sixth."

"All we need now is last year's diary," said Crompton, turning back to the shelves.

"Here we are, Claude! December. December fourth. *Thunder Rock*, Albion Players, seven-thirty, and the initials beside it—"

"H.D.," said Bowden. "Didn't you recognise Davidson's style when you subbed the copy?"

"Seymour probably rewrote it," replied Crompton. "That's what I used to do when I was a junior and wanted to have a night off—get one of the district men to give me a black—y'know, a carbon copy, and then rewrite the thing my own way."

Then he stood and stared at Bowden. "But why, Bowden?"

"That, me learned friend," said Bowden, "is what is taxing the stupendous brains of myself and Reginald Arthur Crossley. There's been a conspiracy of sorts afoot. It could be a matter of wenches only, and it could be more serious, but we have to step like Indians, softlee, softlee. . . ."

He added: "But for that little difficulty we should never have taken you into our confidence. You'll have to act innocence now—and you could have done it much better while you thought you were being chased round. Mind you, you never know, and it's possible we may have to take you in yet! There are no set rules to this game!"

Crompton tapped his fingers on the chair back. "It doesn't make sense, Bowden! It doesn't make sense!"

"A boxful of bits of a jigsaw puzzle don't when you first open the box. That's our job, to put 'em together so's they do make sense. The only snag is that there is no representation of the finished picture on the lid."

He snorted. "Did I say the only snag? The main snag is that we don't get all the bits all at once. There's Mr. Crossley, and me, four detective sergeants, seven d-o's, and about six clerks on this case at the moment—to say nothing of the eight or nine Fleet Street blokes who were anxiously looking for you last night while you were tucked away in your country hideout. *We* knew where you were, but we didn't let on."

"Nice of you," said Crompton.

"Don't kid yourself," Bowden warned him. "We kept quiet for our own benefit, not for yours. We shall try to keep you from them."

"The paper has to come out next week," said Crompton, "and we can't run the thing from Rainley! I think you'll find that if I have one session with them I'll have the coast fairly clear from then on."

"I'm doubtful, but we'll see."

Lisbeth Ann came in with three cups of tea, and the conversation descended to banalities. Bowden eventually left, full of good humour and good fellowship. As he went out Carrington came in, and mounted the stairs two at a time.

"Morning, all!" he greeted them. "What are we going to do today?"

"Glad you called," said Crompton. "I wanted to see you. We're short-handed now. Care to come on the staff for a week or so?"

"I'm on the staff now," said Carrington. "Part owner, aren't I?"

Crompton and Lisbeth Ann exchanged glances.

"According to the lawyers and accountants—not yet," Crompton said sharply. "And when probate is granted Lisbeth Ann will hold the controlling share! No, old cock, you can't have a coronation for some time yet. What we want just now is someone to help out with reporting and rewriting district copy."

"Oh well," Carrington said airily. "May be as well to get my hand in that way as any other. I was thinking of having a go at writing up the lead story for next week."

"And what is the lead story, may I ask?" Crompton asked in a deceptively mild tone.

"Edward John's death, of course! Splash it across the front page, shan't we?"

"You won't! I shall do the story with restraint, and there will be no splashing and no forty-eight-point banner."

"But Packman's policy?"

"We've chopped up the pillory and burned it," said Crompton. "As you were one of the objectors I don't quite understand your present attitude."

"Well, it's dramatic!"

"It's dramatic, but it isn't going to be melodramatic. The sooner you get that idea into your head the better, Charlie. Goodness knows that you vowed against it hard enough when he was alive!"

"Ye-es," Carrington agreed. "It tends to make a difference when you're on the other side of the counter."

"Which you are not, yet."

"You still have to think and plan ahead," Carrington persisted.

"If you're planning on those lines I'll start looking for another job right away," said Crompton. "I'm working for no more Packmans—and I still don't know why I stuck it so long."

"A paper needs to be bright," said Carrington.

"Sure it needs to be bright," Crompton agreed. "There's still a difference between a bright paper and a stinker. So far as the policy of the paper is concerned there'll be two others to have a say in it, you know! You aren't going to be sole owner."

"Doesn't look as if I'm going to be popular, either!" snapped Carrington. "As a writer all these years I consider I've some notion of what the public wants."

"What they want between boards isn't necessarily the same as they want in a paper," Crompton reminded him. "Don't confuse the two markets, Charlie. It could lead to the paper folding up."

Carrington strolled to the door. "Looks as if all my thought about it has been wasted. Oh well, I'll see you on Monday morning! Cheers!"

"Well," said Lisbeth Ann, "if we're going to have that attitude to fight I most certainly shall sell out! I have to choose between the paper and the radio company, anyway."

"There's time yet," replied Crompton. "These are early days in your career. Now we'd better get something done. Will you pack up last week's copy while I collect the proofs?"

Lisbeth Ann went to the reporters' room, and Crompton began to gather the galley and page proofs. The latter he put in page order, and grinned as he looked at the front page he had almost got away with. Packman had almost been beaten!

Then he considered the final version of the front page, and grimaced at the slap-happy make-up. He comforted himself with the thought that it had been made, unmade, and made up again in difficult circumstances.

He riffled through the proofs again, and went down to the works to see if any had been left with Franks. There was none to be found. He looked in the general office, and without calling up to Lisbeth Ann left the building and went round to the police station, to make his way to Crossley's office.

"Come to give yourself up," Crossley asked him humorously.

"I've come to ask a question."

Crossley raised his eyebrows. "Such as?"

"I'd like to know what you found in the general office with Packman's body!"

"Hm? Quite a question!"

Crossley got up and went to the door of Bowden's office. "Can you come through? Mr. Crompton is here."

Bowden gave Crompton his famous stare as he joined them. "What's up?" he asked.

Crompton repeated his question.

"What do you think I found?" asked Bowden.

"The front page proof of the paper."

Crossley and Bowden exchanged glances.

"Why should we be expected to find it?" asked Bowden.

"Because Packman must have been correcting it when he was stabbed!"

"Must he?" stalled Bowden.

"You'll have Baxter's report by now," said Crompton. "That report should tell you whether Packman was standing upright, or bent over the service counter when the knife entered his back."

"Why should he be bending over the service counter?"

"Because the only time any of the editorial staff used that office was on Thursday evenings when the paper was going to bed. It was handier to mark proofs in there than run up and down the stairs with them."

Bowden nodded heavily. "So Packman should have been correcting a page proof. Care to expand the idea?"

"After I'd refused to write the stuff as he wanted it written, he said he'd do it himself. All the others were on jobs, and I'd walked out, so that he would have to do the reading himself. He had written it, because the stuff had been set, and was in the forme. The comps were at break, so that no one but Packman could have set the copy in type, and then put it in the page. The new metal was inked, so that someone had pulled the page. There was nobody but Packman to pull it."

"I thought the page had to be carried across the room to the proofing press," said Bowden. "I've seen 'em do it. Packman couldn't carry one of those things."

"He could ink it with the roller, and then press the paper over it with the dry roller."

Bowden glanced round at Crossley. "He could at that!"

"The page is missing?" said Crossley. "When did you discover this?"

"Just before I came over. I was gathering the proofs together for filing away. All the proofs are there but that one."

There was silence in the room for a few seconds, and Crompton then continued: "I've never stabbed anyone with a knife, but I suppose some blood gets around?"

"It does," Bowden said heavily. "Why?"

"The page would be handy for anyone wishing to wipe a hand, or both hands. Newsprint is highly absorbent."

Bowden put a hand on Crompton's shoulder and led him across the room to the door. "Thanks very much for coming," he said.

Before Crompton was aware of what had happened, he was standing alone in the corridor, staring at the closed door, and from beyond it came the hum of disputing voices.

10
PROOF OF A MURDER

CROMPTON HAD BEEN back at the office no more than ten minutes when Crossley, Bowden, and three detective-officers descended on the building. "Going to turn the place inside out," Bowden explained. "I lost my tiepin when I was here yesterday." Crompton smiled. "Isn't it possible that he folded it and took it with him—to destroy."

Bowden snorted. "Would you walk up the street with a blood-stained sheet of paper in your pocket after you'd just bumped a bloke off? Trouble with you ruddy press fellows is that you lack imagination—can't put yourself in the other fellow's skin. Your job is objective. You report what you see and hear. We have to consider what the criminal thinks and feels. Lot of difference there, cock!"

"That's also the difference between a reporter and a journalist," said Crompton. "The one reports the story, and the other tells the story behind the story."

"If there's a ruddy journalist in this town you can call me Crippen!" snorted Bowden. "If you were as good as you think you are, and you aren't, you'd have been able to help us considerably more than you have done. Unless, of course," he added bitingly, "you don't want to help us!"

"If you're as good as you say you are, then you shouldn't need any help," retorted Crompton. "When are you calling in the Yard?"

"The Yard! I'll break this job open if it kills me!"

"I hope you break it open," said Crompton.

Crossley chuckled, and then asked: "Mr. Crompton, assuming that you had killed Packman, and wiped your hands on the page proof, what would you have done with it afterwards?"

Crompton thought that one out. "Depends how much time I had to spare."

"You'll agree that our man would be in a hurry!"

"And by which door he left the building."

"If he saw Mornington hanging around outside, and managed to dodge him, which he must have done, then he went out through the works."

"In those circumstances," said Crompton, "I should have crammed it well down in the waste-paper sack that hangs on a nail near the works door."

"Now suppose you were in a hurry, and went out over the roof, and dropped into the field behind the building?"

"I can't think of a suitable hiding place in the general office," said Crompton. "That means taking it upstairs with me. And there's nowhere up there. That means taking it out on the roof—and the only possible place to hide it now is in the rain fall-pipes where the gutters between the north-lights empty into them."

"It'd bung them up when it rained," said Bowden. "Not for long," Crompton corrected him. "This newsprint soon disintegrates when it is wetted."

Crossley smiled. "Thanks for your help," he said. "We will now turn the place upside down, and there will be no need for you to stay around."

Crompton took the hint, and together he and Lisbeth Ann went downstairs and out to the yard.

"Care to join me in a spot of something approaching housebreaking," he asked as he turned the scooter and began to push it to the street.

"Will it help?" she asked.

"I can't say," replied Crompton. "I'm going to search Davidson's bed-sitter somehow or other . . ."

"We-ell," Lisbeth Ann said hesitantly. Then she made up her mind, and added: "Let's go!"

Davidson's landlady knew Crompton by sight. She knew that Davidson had gone to Manchester to look for a new job, and she accepted Crompton's story readily when he told her that Davidson had rung through and asked him to get some papers from one of his cases and send them on to him as soon as possible. She allowed them both to go to Davidson's room, and all too trustingly left them to their own devices.

"Well," Lisbeth Ann said brightly when the door had closed behind the landlady, "this is the first time I've been left high and dry in a bedroom with a man!"

"It probably won't be the last," replied Crompton.

"I hope not," she said in such a tone that Crompton looked at her earnest face, and laughed.

"This any good?" she asked, pointing to the bookcase.

"The office key—"

"So he hadn't lost it, Johnny. . . ."

Crompton sat on the edge of the divan bed. "You know, Lisbeth Ann," he said, "there's something darned queer about this business."

"Mr. Crossley seems to be of the same opinion."

She sat close beside him on the bed.

"If Davidson saw that he wasn't making any headway with you, what would be the point in killing your uncle?"

Lisbeth Ann did not know. In fact she did not seem to be interested.

"And what was the point in cutting the cage-bird show? And why did Bill Seymour cut the play after the first act?"

"Ever seen the Fortune Players, Johnny?"

"Bad as that?"

"Worse! Still, Maurice Stanley says they produce the plays for their own amusement."

"But isn't it unlike Bill to dodge a job—or as chief reporter have I been blind to some things that have happened, and some that should have happened and didn't?"

"Bill's pretty conscientious."

"That's what I thought—so why should he cut the play so early?"

Lisbeth Ann looked round the bed-sitting-room. "It's nice here. Quiet and restful, with a sort of intimate atmosphere. . . ."

"Yes," said Crompton, "and if we don't get a move on we shall have the old girl thinking it's too intimate. Landladies have suspicious minds. You turn his wardrobe out while I delve into his suitcases."

Lisbeth Ann sighed, and got on with the work. Ten minutes later they knew they had drawn a blank, and went downstairs to thank the landlady for her kindness.

"I do hope he gets the job," she said. "He never really settled in Carrbank. Pity, too, that he cut his hand like that—and his writing hand as well."

"Cut his hand, did he?" murmured Crompton.

"He'd managed to bandage it up for himself when I got home from the pictures. Said he couldn't get into the office at work for the first-aid box, so he wrapped his hand up in a newspaper to come home. Wasn't that clever!"

"It was very clever," said Crompton, restraining himself. "I suppose he burned the newspaper afterwards?"

"Oh, no. He wouldn't mess my grate up like that, sir. He put it in the dustbin."

"Ah well," said Crompton. "Nice to have a considerate boarder like Harry Davidson. Anyway, thanks, and goodbye."

Outside, as Lisbeth Ann clambered to the rear saddle, he told her to hang on. "It's home, James, and don't spare the horses! I've beaten Bowden to it!"

Bowden and Crossley were interested in Crompton's story. "Gimme that key," said Bowden. "What's the number of the street? Thirty-four? We'll be seeing you, chum."

"Now what?" said Crompton as he watched the two detectives leave.

"I eat on Saturdays," said Lisbeth Ann.

Crompton gave a wry grin. "Suppose it would be a good idea, although I'd rather like to have a word with young Seymour, particularly as he hasn't shown in today. Surely he hasn't bunked off to Manchester to get a job. Anyway, where would you like to go for lunch? The Rialto, or the Oriental?"

"The Quintain at Netherlea. We can get back from there in time to see whether Bill turns up to cover the Carrbank Town match with Winsford."

"Yes, he has that on his slate for today," said Crompton. "All right, you're the boss—or nearly so, so we'll make for Netherlea."

"One plaice and creamed potatoes and blackberry-and-apple pie," said Lisbeth Ann.

"Make it two," said Crompton.

On their return to town they went straight to the football ground. Seymour was not in the press box at the kick-off, so Crompton covered the match, with Lisbeth Ann acting as runner to telephone the game to the paper at the visiting team's town. As the game neared its close Crompton noticed one of Bowden's men waiting near the press-box door. He entered the box as the final whistle went.

"As soon as you can get across, the chief would like a word with you," he said. "He's up at the station."

"As soon as we've sent off the result we'll be there," Crompton assured him, and wasted no time in getting the report finished.

Crossley was pleased to see them. Bowden sat with him, smugly content.

"This isn't an official press conference," Crossley warned them as he waved them to seats. "There are some things you ought to know, and some things we want to know. We spent some considerable time at Davidson's lodging, with interesting results. The key, for instance, which you found. . . ."

"It was lying on the top of the bookcase," said Lisbeth Ann.

"His landlady put it there," said Crossley. "She found it under the bed. With the reluctance most women would display in similar circumstances, she did not like admitting that she only cleaned the room out once a week."

"Was it necessary for her to admit that?" Crompton asked curiously.

Crossley nodded. "We simply had to find out when she discovered it, because there were traces of fluff sticking to it which weren't trouser-pocket fluff. It appears that she came across it after Davidson left for Manchester. He told her he expected to be away for a week, and she admitted that if she got the chance to let the room for odd nights on a bed-and-breakfast basis, she was going to do so, and so she cleaned out the room. The key was lying under the bed-head, right up against the skirting. That sounded odd, until she mentioned that Davidson was in the habit of using the bed-head as a trouser rack. With a little encouragement she had the grace to add that the key was well fluffed, and looked as if it had been there for several days."

"And that invalidates one bright theory," Bowden commented.

Crompton did not answer.

"We found your front page proof, as you suggested, in the dustbin," continued Crossley.

Crompton waited.

"What I am going to tell you now is strictly between ourselves. That understood?"

Both Crompton and Lisbeth Ann nodded.

"There were two sets of finger-prints on it. Nice clear ones. Bloody ones. Delights to a detective's eye. We're checking and rechecking, of course, but there they are!"

"Two sets?" Crompton murmured in a puzzled tone.

"Now try to work out the implications," suggested Crossley quietly. "They are the dabs of Davidson and Seymour. . . ."

"Seymour!" exclaimed Crompton.

"Not Bill!" said Lisbeth Ann.

Crossley nodded. "Davidson and Seymour. Mr. Bowden helped me with the checking. We're sure of it."

Crompton turned to stare at Lisbeth Ann. "That might explain why—"

"Might explain what?" Crossley asked keenly. "You'll find out sooner or later," Crompton said in a weary voice. "Seymour didn't turn up to cover the Town match this afternoon. I had to do it."

Bowden grinned. "Young Mister Seymour done a bunk, Crompton. He got the wind up and bolted home to his mum. He's on his way back to Carrbank now. So is Davidson, under escort."

Crompton chewed his lip, and looked helplessly at Crossley. "Surely a kid like Seymour couldn't get mixed up in a job like that!"

"Danny Moss did," Bowden interposed sharply.

"Yes, I know, but Danny was a different proposition."

"No human being is a different proposition when it comes to murder," Crossley said gently. "The murder impulse and Santa Claus can come to anyone—and in these times the youngsters seem to be handier with knives than adults. They go to the pictures, you know, and watch the big green eye. It wasn't until I had grown up, and been abroad, that I knew how knives were used efficiently. These youngsters are twenty years ahead of people like Bowden and myself. No, Mr. Crompton, I understand your reluctance to believe the possible, but it's there."

"I'm still puzzled by the need to use the page proof," said Crompton. "I didn't think there was so much blood about."

"Your impressions were probably confused," suggested Crossley. "For instance, can you remember even seeing the proof at that time?"

"I can't," Crompton admitted. "As a matter of plain truth I was in too much of a darned hurry to get out. I most certainly got no photographic impression of the scene."

Crossley waved a hand. "You've supplied your own answer."

Crompton shook his head several times. "I still can't believe that Bill Seymour could have been in any way responsible."

"Depends on the quantity and quality of the pressure put on him."

Crompton shrugged. "I'll be quite pleased to meet Harry Davidson once more . . ."

"Please, no!" said Crossley. "Don't add more violence to the dossier."

"Is Seymour coming back under his own steam?"

"British Railways' steam," smiled Crossley. "No escort, if that's what you mean. He didn't run because he's afraid of us, you know, but because he is afraid of Davidson. We've assured him that he has little to fear."

"You've seen him?" Crompton asked, raising an eyebrow.

"We had him met at the other end. He's coming straight back on his return ticket."

"You soon found out that he'd bunked!"

"It's our job to know where all the interested parties are from hour to hour," said Crossley. "This is a murder investigation, Mr. Crompton, and we have a large number of men working on it."

He rose as a sign that the interview was over, and walked slowly round the desk.

"I haven't confided in you and Miss Grosvenor purely for the fun of it, Mr. Crompton. You have a considerable stake in the game, and I am hoping that the information I've given you will refresh your memory—suggest other relevant details which you might care to confide in me later. I'm hoping you will be calling to see *me*."

He showed them out. Lisbeth Ann clutched Crompton's arm as they went slowly down the long red-carpeted corridor to the swing doors and the street.

"I'm—I'm scared, Johnny," she said tremulously. "What was he getting at?"

"I—don't—know," Crompton said hesitantly. "I wouldn't like to say that I'm still not under suspicion. Crossley is as deep as the deep blue sea, and those deep blue eyes are so guileless that I just don't believe 'em! Mr. Crossley is a very clever man, and it's most unpoliceman-like for a man in his position to confide in—well, me!"

He sighed. "Oh well, let's get back to the office. You can amuse yourself in some way or other while I get the match written up. Glory be, but we're like a couple of homeless sparrows, aren't we? Nowhere else to go but to the blasted office—or to impose ourselves on Frances!"

"We are together," Lisbeth Ann said softly.

"That's a lot of comfort!" said Crompton sarcastically.

Lisbeth Ann snatched her arm away. "Oh, men!"

The match did not get written up until Monday, for when they got to the office they found a scared Bill Seymour waiting for them. He greeted them with a tremulous "Hello! I was hoping you'd come in. I'm—I'm sorry about the match, Johnny!"

"We know all about it," said Crompton. "We've just had another interview with the warehouse keepers."

He scratched his head, and regarded Seymour with mock solemnity. "You know, Bill, this must be the craziest newspaper office in Great Britain at the moment. What the hell have you been up to, anyway? How have you managed to get mixed up with Davidson? If you care to open up we can perhaps help you before Crossley lays his manicured fingers on you—or before Bowden's less-genteel maulers grab the scruff of your neck! Or don't you want to talk?"

Seymour did want to talk. He badly wanted to talk, and he badly needed advice.

"It was Davidson's fault, Johnny," he said. "He persuaded me to dodge the play once I'd got the programme and seen the first act. I was to meet him at Greg's place when he got back from Finnerton. He'd got a plan for hanging around until they went for break, and then dodging into the works and defacing the type on four formes so that E.J. couldn't get the paper out this week."

Crompton whistled softly. "I didn't think Davy was upset about Danny! Rather the other way, in fact."

"He wasn't bothered about Danny," Seymour said miserably. "The old man had been taking it out of us all week about Danny's story, and Davy told me he was going to make sure the bloody story never came out at all. Then, afterwards, when I met him at Greg's, he said the whole idea was a neat one to get you blamed for it, and you'd get the sack.

"He waited down the Gate, and got me to wait outside the church and signal to him when the coast was clear. I saw you rush out and go across to the Bells, and then Mornington went for a stroll to the corner of Beck Court. I waved to Davy, and we dodged into the works. We went into the office passage, and Davy tip-toed to the bottom of the stairs to make sure the old man was out of the way. He nodded to me, and then as he turned against the office door . . ."

"Go on," Crompton said grimly.

"Poor Bill!" said Lisbeth Ann.

"We got him off the floor, and there was blood over our hands. When we got him propped up Davy said he couldn't possibly be alive because the blade must have gone in his heart or his lungs. I asked if I should phone the police, and Davy said he'd kill me if I even thought of it again. . . ."

"I'll knock his head off when I see him," said Crompton. "Anyway, get on with the story!"

"Davy said he had a bright idea, and told me to hold the old man up. The sight of him, and all that blood oozing from his back made me go queer. Davy sort of propped him up between the end of the counter and the service counter, and then he belted me half-way across the office. He told me to clear off. Then he changed his mind and said I was to wait. After a minute he told me to go upstairs to the landing, out on the roof through the landing window, and then across the bays and drop into the field at the back. I was then to go straight back to my digs and stay there."

"This is explaining many things," said Crompton. "Press on to the end, my lad. It'll do you good to get it out of your system, and my neck is feeling easier as well."

"I was still feeling a bit weird," continued Seymour, "but Davy said it wouldn't be good for either of us to be found there. He said that the rope that fitted Danny might be accommodated for us. I asked him what he was going to do, and he said he was going to pillory the old bastard like he'd pilloried so many of the burghers of Carrbank. I'd got my hands all over blood—so had he if it comes to that, and asked what I should do. He gave me the page proof to wipe them on, and told me to keep my paws off the window frame as much as I could. So I scrammed back to the digs. The old girl was out, so I went straight to bed. But I didn't sleep. I couldn't. Every time I shut my eyes I could see him. . . . It was the same yesterday, and there was nobody I could talk to, you see, and so I tried to scram off home. And when I got out of the station at the other end there was a plain-clothes man waiting for me. He took me to the station-master's office, told me I might be able to help at this end, and saw me on the next train back."

"Was Davidson sober when all this was happening?" asked Crompton.

"He was about half as tight as a newt, Johnny! He'd had a skinful after leaving the Finnerton young farmers. He knew what he was doing, but he was in that reckless mood of his—you know!"

"I know," said Crompton grimly. "Now, Bill, since you've done a double rail journey we may take it that you haven't much lolly left?"

"I'm about skint, Johnny."

"And when did you eat last?"

"Breakfast."

Crompton took out his wallet, and from it two pound notes. "These aren't a loan, but a present or a gift. I never lend money. Five bob of it is for a good meal, and the rest should see you through until payday next week. Lisbeth Ann will go with you to Greg's place and make sure you order a good tuck-in. When you've had it you are to go straight to the warehouse and ask for Crossley. In the meantime I'll phone him and tell him what's happening. Got it?"

Seymour nodded. "Thanks, Johnny, It's decent of you!"

"Cut it out," said Crompton. "I'm thinking of me. If you want any advice or help after you've seen Crossley I'll be here, or at Mrs. Mundeham's cottage at Rainley—and she's on the phone. Got it?"

Seymour had. Crompton winked at Lisbeth Ann, and she led the lad away. Crompton took up the telephone handset, and dialled the police station.

11
THE LADY IS A SPHINX

AFTER LISBETH ANN and Seymour had gone, Crompton lit a cigarette, put his feet on the desk, and began a mental review of the situation. Whatever opinions he might have held with regard to the efficiency of the local C.I.D. had completely vanished. It was one thing criticising even Murray Bowden when, as a reporter, he was an objective observer, and quite another when he found himself in the middle of the complicated mess that was being investigated. It wasn't even a case of not being able to see the wood for trees; there were apparently no trees. Davidson, while not exactly what might be described as a white sheep, was seemingly innocent of the major crime of killing Packman. He was not even an accessory after the fact, for Packman was well and truly dead when Davidson pilloried him. Who, then, did kill Packman? And for what reason?

At the end of the cigarette he was no nearer any solution, reasonable or otherwise. The only people who benefited by Packman's death were Carrington and Frances Mundeham, and looking at the matter on a long-term basis Frances was a loser, for with Packman's death she had lost the companionship she would have enjoyed if he had lived, and if he had married her.

If he had married her. . . .

Crompton lit a second cigarette, and replayed the section of his mental tape on which was recorded Davidson's comments which had first acquainted Crompton with the existence of Frances Mundeham.

". . . I mean Mistress Frances Mundeham, the cast-off floozie of the late-lamented Edward John . . . her existence in Edward John's life was more or less a secret . . . she was in the habit of waiting round the corner of St. Gudulph's Court with her car. . . . I don't think the penny had dropped on her as yet. Edward John had let his eye fall on the widow woman who runs the Ferryman Inn half a mile below Thorpe Bridge. . . ."

Crompton blew the ash from his cigarette without taking it from his mouth, and murmured: "I wonder!"

It had been done before. It was no new situation for a woman to lead on a man, to coax him into making a will in her favour—or even partly in her favour, and then to kill him. She could have waited at the entrance to St. Gudulph's Court regularly. And from that position she could have watched the works staff leave for break. She could have slipped along the street to the office. She could have got in without being seen—

or without being noticed. In any case, who would bother to notice anyone going into a newspaper office? People were dodging in and out from seven in the morning, when the works staff arrived, until half-past ten at night, when the reporting staff left after writing up night jobs they had done. Mornington was strolling up and down as he waited for the machine to run so that he could collect the copies for the warehouse. She could have left by the front door without being noticed.

Then what had happened inside the office? The paper-knife was part of the office equipment, and had not been taken there for the purpose of killing Packman. Therefore, on the face of it, the killing was unpremeditated.

Crompton seemed to see the whole scene. Packman in the roaring temper which had accompanied him all day, turning on Frances and telling her she was like the rest of them, only interested in him for what she could get out of him. Threatening to change his will. Taking the opportunity to turn her off in favour of "the widow woman who ran the Ferryman Inn below Thorpe Bridge".

Or Frances, having watched the office door and the yard entrance for months, and having pumped Packman into the bargain about the routine on press nights, at last found the opportunity for which she had been waiting—Packman alone, the paper-knife to hand, his back toward her as he bent over the page proof on the service counter. . . .

Both hypotheses were feasible.

And then he remembered Frances's calm acceptance of the fact of Packman's death, and her statement that they must use the scientific method—"Collect all the available facts, and from them form a hypothesis, and later a theory, and then seek to prove the theory. . . . I was once a science mistress in a large school. . . ."

Such a woman was capable of both planning and wait-ing. She accepted tragedy as a fact of life, and accepted life as an adventure. Married to Packman, her adventures would be virtually over. With Packman dead, and his money in her pocket, she was free for further adventures, with her widowhood and peaceful rural setting as aids to her role of innocence.

Crompton stubbed out his cigarette, and grunted. He must see more of Mistress Mundeham, spend more time in her company, look for cracks in the façade.

The door below banged, and Lisbeth Ann scurried past the general office and up the stairs.

"I got a good meal inside him, Johnny, and then saw him right into Crossley's office."

"Good show!" said Crompton.

"And now," said Lisbeth Ann firmly, "you are going to eat!"

Crompton grinned. "It might be a good idea at that. You munched with Bill?"

She shook her head. "I thought I'd go with you."

Crompton glanced at her curiously. "Don't you want to be getting back to Rainley, where you can rest? Frances will get you a meal, and then I can come back into town."

"Well, all right," said Lisbeth Ann. "If you don't mind run-ning me out."

When they arrived at the cottage Crompton went in with her, and Lisbeth Ann, embracing Frances, said: "We're both absolutely starving, Frances!"

"Now look!" Crompton protested. "We agreed that I should run you here, and then go back to town."

"Nonsense," said Frances. "I was expecting you both. Give me ten minutes and you can have grilled steak and chips."

She turned to Lisbeth Ann. "And you can stay here and rest, young lady. I'm getting this meal."

Crompton smiled to himself. Things were going as he had hoped.

"This is cosy," said Lisbeth Ann, curling up on the rug before the log fire. "Won't you draw up your chair?"

"Not on your life," said Crompton. "I don't want to fall asleep and spend another night here. We'll have the villagers talking."

Lisbeth Ann smiled mysteriously. "I don't think you will fall asleep tonight, Johnny, and anyway, you've a large meal to get through yet. You didn't really want to eat in town, did you?"

"We-ell, not really," Crompton admitted, "but I can't keep foisting myself on Frances. Meals cost money, and she hasn't inherited half of Uncle John's fortune yet!"

"Two meals won't break her," said Lisbeth Ann. "Anyway, it gets a bit lonely for her, you know, and she likes company. There's another point, too! What would you have done if you'd gone back to town?"

"We-ell . . ." Crompton answered lamely.

"You'd have had a meal, and then gone to the Falcon with the best intentions!"

"And kept to 'em," said Crompton. "Actually, I wanted to ask a few questions of Morgan and Newnes, and it would have been necessary to keep my head clear."

He paused a moment, and then glanced sharply at her. "So that's why you shanghaied me, is it? Afraid of me going off the wagon again?"

Lisbeth Ann stared into the fire. "You're nice when you're sober, Johnny. You get cynical and sarcastic when you've had a few, and it doesn't suit you."

"I've only myself to please," Crompton retorted.

"If you hadn't raved off at Uncle John the other night, and gone to get nearly stewed at the Falcon. . . ."

"I know! I know!" said Crompton. "Uncle John would be alive today! I should have been at the office writing up foul copy like a good and obedient servant, and nobody would have been able to kill him. God, isn't that just like a woman!"

"When you two have finished falling out there's a meal waiting in the dining room," said Frances from the doorway.

As they followed her to the dining room she added: "You can't afford to fall out, you know. You're temporarily dependant on each other."

"I'm not dependant on anyone," said Crompton. "I can go and get myself a job in London, Manchester, or Birmingham tomorrow!"

"It's Sunday tomorrow, Johnny Crompton!" she countered.

"Well, on Monday, then!"

Frances chuckled. "You'd better ask Mr. Crossley about that, my lad!"

"You mean that he's still—"

"Suspecting you? No-o, I wouldn't say that, but you are a material witness, and the police don't like witnesses to get lost. Take Davidson for instance . . . !"

"Just a minute," Crompton said sharply. "What do *you* know about Davidson getting—er—lost?"

She smiled at him. "Mr. Crossley called on me this morning. He mentioned it during the course of a somewhat long and interesting conversation."

Crompton saw an opening. "Mr. Crossley's very interested in you, isn't he? You weren't in Carrbank on Thursday night, were you?"

She gave him the sphinx-like smile again. "I told you I wasn't, Johnny! I told you I never waited at St. Gudulph's Court like a schoolgirl waiting for her first beau. Edward was paying court to me—and I was definitely not running after him!"

"Sorry!" said Crompton. "Mannerless of me to ask!"

"If you'll only take your seats at the table we can eat. I'm absolutely starving. I expected you both for lunch, and apart from a very light tea I've had nothing since my breakfast!"

"We had to cover the match," said Lisbeth Ann.

Frances nodded. "I know! Bill Seymour had run home to his mum."

"That's what Bowden said!" Crompton exclaimed.

Frances smiled amiably. "Yes, he came to see me after Mr. Crossley left."

"There's a mystery here somewhere," grunted Crompton, and said his thanks as she passed his plate.

"No mystery at all," she replied. "It's best English silverside, with potatoes and kidney beans grown in my own garden."

"What's the use!" murmured Crompton, raising his eyes to the oak beams.

"Exactly," said Frances. "What's the use! You know, Johnny Crompton, you still suspect me, don't you?"

"Who, me?" Crompton asked.

Frances chuckled, and shook her head. "You're as transparent as a glass pane. Now listen, Johnny. I have a sound alibi for every minute of Thursday evening from five o'clock until bedtime. Both Mr. Crossley and Inspector Bowden know of it, they have checked it, and so you can cross me from your list."

"Then who the devil was it!" exclaimed Crompton.

"So you did suspect me!" she said quickly.

"Johnny!" Lisbeth Ann said in a shocked voice.

The rest of the meal was eaten in silence. Frances wore an amused smile throughout it, Lisbeth Ann glowered at Crompton, and Crompton continually sniffed his embarrassment.

Later, Frances said she would serve coffee in the lounge. As Crompton and Lisbeth Ann waited there he poked the fire, cleared the bars, and put two logs on the embers.

"Somebody killed him," he said at last.

"Well, it wasn't Frances!" Lisbeth Ann said defiantly.

"No," Crompton agreed. "It wasn't Frances. She has an alibi. . . ."

"There are just odd times when you're hateful, Johnny!" said Lisbeth Ann.

"Tonight's one of 'em," said Crompton. "I hate having a question in my mind that I can't answer. It's frustrating!"

Frances came in with the tray. "What is?" she asked.

"Not knowing the answer."

"It surely isn't your job to find the answer, is it?" she said. "You're a journalist, not a detective. Mr. Crossley and Inspector Bowden are quite capable, I can assure you!"

"You know more than I do," said Crompton.

"That's possible—about some things, but taking me all round I'm not too bright."

"And what might that mean?"

Frances shrugged. "Anything—or nothing."

They sat quietly for some time, sipping the coffee. The silence of the cottage was broken by the shrilling of the telephone bell from the hall. Frances laid her cup and saucer aside and went to answer it.

She was gone about five minutes, and when she came back she sat down and looked at them thoughtfully.

Lisbeth Ann laid a hand on her knee. "Something wrong, dear?"

"It was Mr. Crossley. Davidson is on the run. He got away from the detective—laid him out with one good punch that knocked his head against the carriage window while the train was standing in the station at Sheffield. He made an unnoticed exit from the station, and, well, he's on the loose!"

Crompton fed the fact into his brain, and then said: "It makes one wonder whether Davy hasn't a bigger stake in the game than we've suspected!"

"Than you've suspected," said Frances.

"There's another point," said Crompton. "Why should Crossley tell you?"

"It was necessary, Johnny," she replied, and offered no further explanation.

"I give up," said Crompton.

"Very wise, Johnny," Frances commented.

"How long had you known Edward John?"

"Two and a half years and five weeks."

Crompton did some elementary mental arithmetic. "That would be April three years ago," he said.

"It isn't significant, surely?"

"No, it doesn't mean anything really," Crompton replied. He waved a loose hand. "I'm just trying to collect facts, you know."

"He was attending a conference in London, and I was in London on business, and we stayed at the same hotel. Care to know which hotel it was?" she asked with a puckish smile.

"Eh? No, of course not."

"I was in town to see an editor."

Crompton was silent.

"I write country articles for *Country World.*"

"You do!"

"Me!"

Frances smiled.

"And for the past eighteen months I've done the nature notes for the *Borough News*—anonymously."

Crompton scratched his head. "I always thought they were syndicate stuff," he said lamely. "Don't seem to know much about my own paper, do I?"

"They are generally regarded as fill-up, aren't they?" said Frances. "I believe there's a very rude name for them in most weekly paper offices. Anyway, in that Pimlico hotel I recognised Edward John Packman, and I deliberately made myself known to him with the object of selling him my idea for a nature column. That was the only occasion when I've tried deliberately to get anything from him."

She gave the puckish smile again. "I wonder if the new editor will want the 'Life In The Country' feature . . . Anyway, the first three articles gave Edward the idea that the country could supply the peace of mind he couldn't find in town—and that is why he began visiting me. I think he believed I worked from nature books and the encyclopaedia, and so I led him through the meadows and woods—and not up the garden path, Johnny!"

"You're being grossly unfair to me," Crompton protested.

"Oh no!" she replied. "You are like some of the people in this village—you can't understand anyone doing anything for anyone else, even to showing them friendship, without getting something out of it. This tragedy will prove a valuable experience to you, Johnny Crompton. You had reached the point where people are just names on paper, lacking life, mere walking robots, people to be pursued because they could provide a story."

Crompton made a gesture of protest, but Frances continued: "And what do you get for it? You write all week, and think you have produced death-defying prose. You get into a sweat and a temper on press night—as Edward did—and when you walk down the street on Friday morning you see housewives using the *Borough News* as wrapping for their fish or meat.

"And all you are doing is satisfying two very elementary human urges—for people to see their own names in print, and for people to pry into the lives of others. You are the man sitting on a wall, telling the people on one side of it how the people on the other side are behaving to their friends and relatives. Week after week your front-page headlines tell how Man Beats Dog To Death or how Unconscious Girl Was Raped. And if there are no heads like that in the *News* you apologise to your friends because the paper happens to be dull that week!"

"This—this is ridiculous!" said Crompton, rising from his chair.

"It's also slanderous, but it happens to be true. Stir the least-worthy emotions of your readers and you are a good reporter. You don't think in terms of human stories, but in terms of good headlines. When that awful character threw his dog into a sludge-filled and disused quarry last winter, and the dog was rescued by a fireman, you dealt first with the evil action of the man, and then with the plight of the dog, and the fireman's heroism came in a poor third."

"If you'll excuse me I'll be getting back to town," said Crompton.

He went to the hall for his overcoat and crash helmet, and was letting himself out when Frances followed him to the door.

"You must come again, Johnny," she said. "Next time you should not come with the intention of proving to yourself that I am guilty of murdering the man I loved. You're a good reporter, but a very poor actor! Good-night!"

Crompton closed the door without answering. He got the scooter from behind the cottage, and drove too quickly back to town, and straight to the C.I.D. headquarters.

One of the divisional sergeants was in the corridor as he walked in. "Looking for Mr. Crossley?" he said.

Crompton nodded. "Or Bowden."

"They're both out on the job. Suppose you've heard about it?"

"I've been on it for months now—or does it only seem like months," Crompton said bitterly.

"Oh, I don't mean Packman's job. We've a new one."

"What's this?" Crompton asked quickly.

"Old Townley, the gunsmith. Somebody broke into his workshop tonight—about an hour ago. Townley disturbed him, and got shot through the guts for his trouble. He's on the op table at the hospital now—and judging by the preliminary report his chances aren't too good."

"Davidson!" exclaimed Crompton.

"We aren't saying that. In fact we aren't saying anything, but there's nothing to connect the two—as yet!"

"You never do say anything," said Crompton. "The Press could help a great deal more than they do if they were given the chance."

"Blowing the gaff never helped anybody," said the sergeant. "By the way, your pal Carrington was here on the same errand as yourself twenty minutes ago. Bowden gave him the rough edge of his tongue."

"That's the only edge he's got," said Crompton. "Do you know where he is now? Carrington, I mean."

"Said he was going to your office to look for you."

"Thanks," said Crompton. He went outside and mounted the scooter.

Carrington was just leaving the office by the front door as Crompton drew into the kerb.

"Heard about the Townley business?" he asked.

Crompton nodded. "I've just been to the warehouse. Know anything about it?"

"I may do soon," said Carrington, lowering his voice. "If you can stick around here for about an hour I may be able to phone something through to you. In fact I may need your help—but I must know where to find you!"

"It's now nine o'clock," said Crompton, glancing at the clock of St. Gudulph's Church. "I'll slip into the Bells for a couple of glasses, and then mount guard in the office. How long do you want me to hang on?"

"Half-ten be too late?"

Crompton shrugged. "Not if there's a story. I've damn-all else to do or go."

"You'll be hearing from me then," said Carrington, and walked briskly up the Gate.

12

THE TERROR BY NIGHT

For an hour Crompton stooged around the offices, and then sat down. By half-past ten he had fallen asleep, and when the telephone aroused him he glanced at his watch and saw that it was half-past two in the morning. He silently cursed Carrington, and lifted the handset from the cradle. "Where the hell have you been, Charlie?" he demanded sleepily. "Don't I see enough of this office without having to start a night shift?"

"It's me—Lisbeth Ann," said a scared voice on the line. "We've been locked in our room, and we've had burglars. The cottage has been turned inside out. Can you come out to us?"

"I'm on my way," said Crompton. He ran down the stairs to the yard and his scooter. Two night-patrolling policemen noted his number and his approximate speed as he passed them, and his progress and direction had been passed on by telephone to Crossley's office long before he pulled up at the cottage gate.

He walked quickly to the front door and opened it. Lisbeth Ann almost fell into his arms. "Oh, Johnny, it was awful!"

Crompton pushed her before him into the lounge, where Frances was standing in a wrecked room with a strange and twisted smile on her face.

"Ever see such a mess, Johnny Crompton? Every drawer in the house has been pulled on the floor and its contents scattered."

"What about the room you were in?" asked Crompton. Then he said: "You'd better tell me the story from the start."

"Come into the kitchen with me. I'm going to make coffee. It started half an hour after you left. I usually go for a stroll along the lane before I go to bed. I've done that for years. Lisbeth Ann came with me, of course. We were out about twenty minutes to half an hour. When we got back we found my bedroom turned inside out, and like the three bears we looked round the house and found Lisbeth Ann's room had been similarly served."

"You phoned the police?"

She shook her head. "No, perhaps it was a mistake, but I fancied that we'd have no further interruption, and I didn't relish the police being here all night, taking finger-prints, and statements, and generally keeping us from sleep. So we locked up and went to bed. Lisbeth Ann came into my double bed. We put a chair under the door-knob, and that was that!"

She busied herself with the percolator, and continued: "It would be three-quarters of an hour ago that Lisbeth Ann awoke me. Someone was moving about downstairs. I have a small revolver—-and no licence for it, so I loaded it, took the chair away, and tried to open the door. It was then we discovered that the key was on the outside—!"

"Someone with brains," commented Crompton. "That must have been done on the first visit. It's somebody who knows your movements."

"Don't let's talk like policemen," said Frances. "It certainly looks as if the raid was planned in two stages, but anyway

I got out by the simple method of unscrewing the lock-box with a nail-file, and although I was as quiet as I could be our visitor had gone by the time we crept downstairs. Somehow I still didn't fancy sending for the police, and so I worked on a hunch provided by Lisbeth Ann, who said she didn't think you'd go back to your digs, and would probably be sleeping rough in the office."

Crompton leaned against the kitchen wall. "Look, Frances," he said, "where do you fit into this affair? What is there you possess that would justify a thorough search like this?"

"I've nothing of such value," she said soberly.

"Why is Crossley so interested in you?"

"I can't tell you, Johnny," she replied.

"You mean you won't tell me, or you aren't at liberty to tell me!"

"Surely you must realise that as Edward's wife-to-be I knew a great deal about his affairs, and Mr. Crossley obviously wishes to know all he can about those affairs?"

"Yes, I see that," said Crompton. "The fact that sticks out a mile is that there is something you know which somebody regards as highly important!"

"That I can't say, Johnny. Someone murdered Edward, and that somebody must have had a reason—a motive—for doing so. Come along, we'll take the coffee to the lounge."

"We should tell the police, you know," said Crompton.

"Yes, I realise that," she nodded. Then she cocked an ear. "I rather fancy someone is coming along the village in a car."

"Two policemen were interested in my speed as I came here," said Crompton. "Yes, the car's drawing in. . . ."

Frances went to the door and opened it. Crossley and Bowden were walking hurriedly up the path.

"Crompton here?" asked Crossley.

"You know he is," Frances said quietly. "Isn't that his scooter beside your car. Anyway, do come in. I was just going to phone you."

The two detectives followed her into the lounge, and stood in the doorway looking round at the mess.

"Morning!" said Crompton.

They ignored him.

"Starting to flit?" asked Bowden sarcastically.

"We've had a visitor," Frances replied. "If you'll wait while I make more coffee I'll tell you about it."

She hurried back to the kitchen.

"Only this room?" asked Crossley.

"Every room in the house," said Lisbeth Ann. "Someone locked us in our room."

"We're listening," Bowden said heavily, so Lisbeth Ann told them the whole story.

"Found Davidson?" Crompton asked when Lisbeth Ann had finished.

"We haven't—yet," Bowden said in a sour voice. "You any bright ideas about where he might be?"

"Not unless he's already been," replied Crompton, indicating the disorder around them.

"Oddly enough, that had occurred to me," said Bowden.

Crossley had drawn a pair of gloves on his hands, and was walking about the room inspecting the escritoire, the china cabinet, and other pieces of highly polished furniture.

"We'll have to do the routine," he said after a while, "but I think our man wore gloves. That means he's no casual character merely looking for odds and ends of cash."

"I'm interested in Mrs. Mundeham's connection with Packman's death," Crompton said in a flat voice.

"Who isn't?" murmured Crossley. He smiled, and added: "Yes! Who isn't! That's a very good question." As Frances returned he said:—"You won't mind having a couple of men in for a couple of hours, searching for possible finger-prints?"

"Will it matter whether I mind or not?" she smiled. "No, not really, Mr. Crossley. I rather fancy the idea of a guard between now and dawn."

"And you don't know what the intruder was after?" asked Bowden.

"She doesn't," said Crossley.

"Seems to me," went on Bowden, "that somebody's looking for something, and isn't quite sure where it is. We'll find 'em, and we'll find it! For now I'll fetch Tomlinson and Carter to go over the furniture, and then I'll see if it's possible to sleep for half an hour."

"That's an idea," said Crompton. "If no one requires my presence I'll get back to the office and finish my nap. Sometimes I wonder why I ever try to sleep at all."

"I can't expect you to—er—kip down on the settee while the detectives are upsetting the place," said Frances, "but if you care to turn up in time for breakfast, about nineish, I suggest you spend the day with us. I can perhaps take us all for a run in the car later on."

"Please do, Johnny!" said Lisbeth Ann.

"Thanks, I'll do that," said Crompton.

He lifted an eyebrow to Crossley. "Okay?"

"Okay," said Crossley.

Crompton set off back to town. He ran the scooter through the deserted streets and into the yard. As his headlight shone on the whitewashed wall he was aware of something wrong, something different. He disengaged the gears, and stopped the engine. As he put his right foot to the floor splinters of glass crunched under it. He swung the handlebars to the right, and it was then he saw that a glass pane in the door was broken, and the works door was wide open.

"Oh heck! Again!" he exclaimed.

It never occurred to him that the breaker-in might still be on the premises. He put the scooter on its stand, and stepped inside the works. He found the switch with his left hand, and pressed it down. Then he caught his breath, for lying across the floor was the constable, Mornington. His helmet was lying some distance away, and there was blood under the man's head.

Crompton bent over him, and felt his pulse. It was beating feebly. He stepped over him and hurried to the phone in the general office. There were two lines, so he took both receivers from the cradles, and in turn dialled 999 and Frances's number. The police call was answered first, and he rapidly told what little story he had to tell. Then he heard Frances answering, and merely asked her to tell Crossley and Bowden to hurry back to town, and the *News* office.

He returned to Mornington, raised him up, and propped him against his knee. He examined the back of his head. There was a cut about an inch long, and a large bump surrounding it. He had been coshed. He slipped from his coat and doubled it up as a pillow for Mornington, and then laid him down again.

Then he went upstairs, switching on lights as he went. He knew what to expect, and was not disappointed.

Packman's desk had been ransacked, and consequential and inconsequential papers were spread over the floor. He looked into each room on the landing, and then went downstairs to keep an eye on Mornington, and to await the police.

There was something of a bother when the night inspector and two sergeants arrived. The welfare of a British citizen is important to the police; the safety of a policeman is of paramount importance.

"The so-and-so won't get away with this!" said the inspector angrily. "Get on the blower and get Dr. Burrows out of bed, Jackson. Blimey, poor old Moray's out cold!"

He stood up and looked hard at Crompton. "And where would you be round about the time that Mornington was coshed?"

"With Mr. Crossley and Murray Bowden at Rainley," Crompton said softly. "You can't tie this on to me! You should know the time of his last conference point, or when he reported to the office by phone, and so you should be able to put a time on the assault. While you're here, you should have a look upstairs."

"What's upstairs?" asked the inspector.

"That's another good question that you might ask of Mr. Crossley when he arrives. He'll be here within the next few minutes. I took the liberty of phoning him."

The inspector grunted.

Crossley, Bowden, and the doctor arrived within two minutes of each other. Mornington was sent to hospital still unconscious, with a suspected fractured skull, and the sixteen-inch-long spanner that lay two feet away was carefully wrapped in a waste copy of the *News* and taken away for examination.

Then Crossley took Crompton upstairs, and waved toward the desk. "In which pigeon-hole, or in which drawer did he keep really private papers?" he asked.

"To the best of my knowledge and belief he didn't keep any private papers at the office," said Crompton. An idea occurred to him, and he told Crossley so.

"What is it?" asked Crossley.

"If he had any private papers—and what man hasn't—wouldn't he be more likely to keep them at his home?"

Crossley smiled wryly. "Oddly enough, I had thought of that. We have a policeman on duty night and day there."

"He could also be coshed," said Crompton. "Our man does seem to be making a night of it, doesn't he?"

"You need convincing," said Crossley. "Ring the house—not from this instrument. Use that in your own room."

He gave a grin. "If you don't get a reply, do please let me know!"

Crompton went along the corridor to his own room. Four minutes later he went back and announced simply: "Mr. Crossley, there is no reply from Packman's house."

Crossley put a hand over his eyes, and groaned. "Bowden," he said, "if that man of yours is having a crafty sleep I'll have his uniform off his back. And if he isn't we'll need the ambulance. Get cracking, man!"

Bowden vanished, cursing loudly that he'd soon not have a man left at the warehouse. Crossley indicated that he wished Crompton to stay with him, and for the next half-hour Crompton told him what he could expect to find among the documents from various drawers, while Crossley steadily pumped him for details of Packman's business life.

It was at the end of the half-hour that Bowden's large and weary feet were heard plodding up the stairs.

"Two policemen in dock now," he announced stolidly.

"And the place ransacked?" Crossley said quietly.

Bowden nodded.

"We'll need more men from county headquarters," said Crossley. "What was the manner of entering at Packman's place?"

"Townsley's still unconscious, but we found him in the back yard. Looks as if somebody had got him to the door. . . ."

"That only leaves Carrington," commented Crossley.

"Why, Crossley?" asked Crompton.

Crossley consulted his wrist watch before answering. "Two hours to dawn. Care to see prophecy reduced to a fine art?"

He nodded to Bowden. "Come on. You also come with me, Mr. Crompton—and don't bother me with questions."

Outside they got into the car, and Crossley drove through the centre of the town. "Guide me now. I only know the general direction of Carrington's house."

As they neared the residential district in which Carrington lived they saw a policeman pedalling furiously in the same direction as themselves.

"What did I tell you!" said Crossley.

He drove alongside the policeman, and flagged him to dismount. "Tell me," he said simply.

"Somebody been in at Carrington's house—the writer bloke, sir."

"Leave your bike against the kerb, and hop in," said Crossley.

Charlie Carrington was standing on his front doorstep in dressing gown and slippers, with the legs of a pair of orange pyjamas flapping in the light breeze.

"Never saw such a mess in your life!" he greeted them. "All my papers turned inside out, and two bound manuscripts torn apart."

"What time was it?" Crossley asked in what appeared to be an uninterested voice.

"Not half an hour ago."

"Anything missing?"

"Not unless he took a fancy to a few odd pages of my new novel."

"He's a mug if he did," commented Bowden.

"Where's your wife?" asked Crossley.

"Keeping warm in bed."

"I'd like to see her," said Crossley.

"Well," Carrington said with a shrug. "I'll take you up if you insist."

"Down here!" Crossley said. He watched every step that Carrington made as he went upstairs.

"Thinking of something?" asked Bowden.

Crossley turned slowly, and nodded. "Yes, Bowden, I'm thinking of something. . . ."

He prowled round the room, seemingly seeing everything visible, and things that other people could not see. There was a whisky bottle on the table, and beside it an empty glass. He wrapped his handkerchief round his fingers, and carefully lifted the glass. He slid it into his pocket as Cora Carrington bustled down the stairs, wrestling with a boudoir wrap that was determined to win.

She was in her late thirties, and her hair was dyed to the colour of unripe corn. Her makeup was as intact as if she had just renovated it, and two light brown pencilled eyebrows rose like cantilever arches across her high forehead.

As she flapped across to them in scarlet mules the wrap won, and fell away from her nightdress.

"I was just going to have a bath!" she said in a high-pitched voice.

"Sure you weren't in it?" asked Bowden, scanning the scanty nightwear.

She glanced down at her body. "I'm not ashamed of the body, but you don't look as if you've ever been interested in anything but dead ones. Charlie-boy's the devil for them—this one at any rate. At the going down of the sun he thinks of little else, and he's the same in the morning. Age cannot wither, nor custom stale, his infinite interest—"

"Shurrup!" said Carrington.

"We didn't ask you to come down for a discussion on sex," Crossley said mildly. "We want to know if you heard anything of the intruder?"

She dug her finger tips into her breast. "Me? I go out like a light once my head's on the pillow. I heard nothing until Charlie dug me in the ribs and said he could hear noises. I thought he'd been dreaming, of course, but he came back a minute or so later and said we'd had burglars."

"At what time did you go to bed?"

She looked at her husband. "What time was it, Charlie?"

"Well," said Carrington. "You went up about eleven, and I stayed up to finish my chapter. I got in bed—oh, probably about quarter past twelve."

Crossley waved a hand around. "Only this room disturbed?"

"Only this," replied Carrington.

"Any idea what the intruder might have been looking for?"

"Money, I suppose," Carrington replied. "I've nothing of value in the place, really. No valuable paintings nor other objets d'art. And we never keep much money in the house. There have been a good many breakings-in around this area during the past two autumns and winters, as you know."

"That's so," Crossley said absently. He appeared to be looking for something, for his eyes continually roved about the room.

He suddenly turned back to Carrington. "If he was looking for money, what would be his object in tearing your manuscripts to pieces?"

"Hm?"

"You heard my question," said Crossley.

"Well, I don't know," Carrington replied lamely.

"Just shows," said Bowden. "The detective writer can't think of one sensible answer when it comes to the real thing. He didn't come in for a warm, I suppose? Or to ask you how to write thrillers?"

"Seen or heard anything of Davidson?" Crossley asked casually.

"I'm not a detective," Carrington replied. "Mr. Bowden should know more about Davidson than I do."

"Perhaps I do," said Bowden. "This is another occasion when me know how."

Crossley apparently decided that the show was at an end. He tapped Bowden on the arm. "You stay here until the dabs boys arrive."

He gestured toward the whisky bottle. "You been having a tot of that tonight, Mr. Carrington?"

Carrington looked at the bottle as if it was the first time he had noticed it. "No-o," he replied. "It should have been in the cocktail cabinet over there."

Crossley nodded. He took Crompton by the arm. "I'd like you to travel back to town with me. There are several points about your office routine I haven't got clear in mind yet. Good-night, all."

He never spoke a word to Crompton all the way back to town, and when they reached the police station he indicated that he was to follow him inside. He sat him down in his office and threw a packet of cigarettes and his lighter on the table. "Wait until I get back, Mr. Crompton."

Twenty minutes later he returned. There was a tightness about his mouth that Crompton had never seen there before. He sat at the opposite side of the desk, and stared hard at him.

"The next few hours will be vital ones, Mr. Crompton. I've had certain suspicions for a long time now—as time goes in these cases. . . ."

He was silent for a few moments, and then he sighed.

"You know, Mr. Crompton, I sometimes wish I'd been a bullfighter instead of a policeman. The bull-fighter has a distinct advantage over a policeman—particularly over a detective policeman. He experiences the supreme moment of truth when the killing-sword goes between the shoulders of the bull into its heart. He knows then that he has finished the job. We policemen are really only the picadors or whatever they call 'em who get the bull ready for the legal characters to finish off. . . ."

He reached for the cigarettes, lit one, and blew the smoke down his nostrils.

"There should be such moments for a policeman, but there never is," he continued. "What should be the moment of truth comes either before or after the arrest. The climax for the victim, for Mr. Packman, is the moment when he realises that death is inevitable. The climax for the murderer may be the moment when he is acquitted, or sentenced to prison, or when he stands on the trap with his legs together. In either case he knows he has reached the end of the ordeal. . . ."

"Why are you saying this?" Crompton asked in a gentle voice.

Crossley gave a wry smile. "There are so few people I can talk to in this way. That is why I appreciate the company of Mrs. Mundeham. You like Frances Mundeham, Crompton?"

"She's a lady," replied Crompton.

Crossley leaned over the table. "There are some things I want to tell you. The finger-print tests are by no means complete, but I've made my guesses—or deductions if you like—and I'm telling you that no 'foreign' prints will be found in Mrs. Mundeham's cottage, nor at Packman's house, nor in your office. The prints on the glass I whipped away from Carrington's house belong to one person only—Harry Davidson!"

"So he got back to town!"

"He got back to town, Crompton!"

Crossley twisted the cigarette between his fingers until it was a mere smoking twisted mess.

"You didn't say whether you liked Mrs. Mundeham or not."

"I do like her. She's a lady."

"In that case," said Crossley, "I'd accept her invitation and go round for breakfast—and stay all day—and then stay all night!"

"You mean . . . ?"

"I mean," said Crossley, "that she's in danger, real danger of losing her life. You're an intelligent man, Crompton, and even if you don't know the reason—and I'm most certainly not going to tell you—you've realised that she is the fulcrum of this case. The hub is the better description, for everything revolves around her. She's safe in the daylight hours, but once night falls anything might happen."

He smiled at Crompton. "I know you've no place to lay your head, and like me you're a bachelor, so let's go down to the canteen and see if we can find a cup of tea and a bite. Then you can borrow one of the bunks until half-past eight in the morning—but be at Rainley for nine o'clock, please!"

13
THE WIDOW AT THE FERRYMAN

SUNDAY MORNING breakfast was a cosy affair for Crompton. The morning ride in the frosty air gave him an appetite which was well satisfied by a plate of bacon, sausage, liver, and egg. A log fire was burning brightly in the hearth, and both Frances and Lisbeth Ann appeared, temporarily, at least, to have forgotten the tragedy. They were both in conversational moods, and Crompton had no sense of being an interloper—although he gave a rueful smile as he realised that once Crossley and company had rounded up Packman's murderer his life was likely to return to the routine of lodgings, work, and the Golden Falcon. And he was quite sure he did not want that type of existence any longer. On the other hand he could not see any possibility of any other kind of life opening up to him.

"You're pensive, Johnny!" said Frances.

Crompton looked up and smiled. "Hm? Sorry, I was dreaming. . . ."

"Probably in love," Frances nodded. "Young men do become pensive at such times."

"Not me!" said Crompton. "I can't say that I've ever been in love. Odd temporary infatuations and all that, but never serious."

"Obviously not the type," said Lisbeth Ann, keeping her eyes turned down to the table.

"I always seem to have to be too much concerned with work," Crompton mumbled.

"We shall have to find means of letting you escape from it more when we re-organise," said Lisbeth Ann.

Frances raised a fine-pencilled eyebrow, and remained silent. After a few moments she said: "Johnny must have time to write."

More briskly she added: "You can laze about all morning while Lisbeth Ann and I prepare lunch, and then I propose having a run out in the car."

"Where to?" asked Crompton.

"Oh, up or down the river—preferably down, away from Carrbank, and then we can perhaps spend an hour at the Ferryman."

Crompton laid down his knife and fork. "The Ferryman? What in heaven's name for?"

"Oh, I'd rather like a chat with the merry widow."

"There's something behind this," said Crompton.

"Of course there is—and haven't you guessed what it is?"

Crompton shook his head.

Frances reached a hand across the table. "More coffee? You'll have all morning and afternoon to think it out, Johnny. By the way, you can fight if it becomes necessary?"

"Who with? The widow?"

"By what I know of her, Johnny, a handsome young man like you wouldn't even have to wrestle with her! However, we'll leave the whole thing for now."

Crossley appeared shortly after eleven o'clock, and after half an hour's private conversation with Frances he entered the lounge and closed the door behind him.

"Spare a minute?" he asked Crompton. "There's a question. . . . When you left the Falcon to go back to the office on Thursday night, by which door did you leave?"

"Why, the Market Square entrance—or exit."

"It's the longest of the three ways out."

"Yes, it is, but it's a matter of habit—so much so that Okky says I only use the place as a means of cutting off the corner. I always enter from the Gate, and go out into the Square. Dunno why, but it's just one of those things."

Crossley sucked a tooth, and looked hard at Crompton. "You then have to walk round two sides of the block!"

"Yes."

"Now tell me something else if you can. The paper-knife; does it always lie on the table in the general office?"

"Well, ye-es, I suppose it does—either there or somewhere handy for the girls to open the mail with."

"So that you'd know it was all nice and handy if it had been you that went in to knife Packman?"

"Ye-es, I suppose I should if I'd thought it out."

"There's another paper-knife on Packman's roll-top desk, one with a black handle. Can that always be found there?"

"It's been on his desk ever since I joined the firm."

"So that whether Packman was upstairs or down, someone who knew the office would know there was a knife handy?"

"I suppose I have to say yes to that also."

"Now I want to ask you another. When the men break on press nights, does Franks always drop the latch on the door of the works?"

"I've never known him do it yet," said Crompton. "I don't have to tell you that we do night jobs, and when I've come in on Thursday nights I've always cut through the works to save fiddling in my pockets for my key to the front door."

Crossley stroked his chin. "Now there's a thing!" he said.

"Heard anything of Davidson yet?" asked Crompton.

"We haven't heard of him, or from him."

"What happened about Bill Seymour?"

"Seymour? Oh yes, we had a little chat with him. Very observant and interesting lad is Seymour. I think he'll make a good reporter, Crompton."

"I'll tell him that in the morning," said Crompton. "It'll buck him up no end."

Crossley walked to the door. "I'll go if you're going to get sarcastic. By the way, Crompton, don't forget that I asked you to stay overnight!"

"I'll need to be invited first," said Crompton.

"I've already fixed that," replied Crossley. "Mrs. Mundeham thinks it's a good idea—oddly enough not for the reason I suggested."

"What other reason could there possibly be?"

Crossley put his hands on his hips and grinned. "Seymour's a better reporter than you are, Crompton. He notices things, and I'm blessed if you can see further than the end of your nose. Cheerio!"

"There are more mysteries than one in these parts," Crompton said to the closed door.

Lisbeth Ann joined him a few minutes later. She seated herself on a pouffe by the fire, and rested her chin on her hand, and her elbow on her knee.

"When will you teach me to drive the scooter, Johnny?"

"We'd perhaps better wait until you've got a provisional licence and your insurance fixed up. I've no wish to appear in Borough Court for aiding and abetting."

"Then you will!"

"I promised, didn't I?" asked Crompton.

She nodded. "Yes, but you haven't mentioned it since we went to Fogg's garage and picked the machine."

"Probably had one or two other things in my mind," said Crompton. "By the way, what has Frances got in her mind about the widow at the Ferryman?"

Lisbeth Ann shook her head. "I don't think anyone ever knows what Frances has in mind. Her husband must have had a fine time with her—but whatever she makes up her mind to do is done! And while the questioning is on, can I ask what Crossley wanted?"

"I don't know what he wanted from Frances—"

"He only wanted to see her," Lisbeth Ann interrupted.

"—but he wanted to know by which exit I left the Falcon when I went back to the office."

Lisbeth Ann stared wide-eyed at him for a long time, and then she shook her head slowly, and said in a shocked voice: "Oh no!"

"Oh no, what?"

"Not—not that!"

Crompton laughed. "What on earth is biting you? What do you mean?"

Lisbeth Ann continued to stare at him, and then again shook her head very slowly from side to side. "You wouldn't believe me, Johnny. We'd better skip it."

"I'm loving this," said Crompton. "Crossley, Frances, and now you! You all treat me like a child who wouldn't understand a long word if it was told to him."

"Well, perhaps you wouldn't—so what?"

She suddenly jumped up, ruffled his hair playfully, and ran from the room, laughing.

"Any minute now I'm going out to have myself certified," Crompton called after her.

After lunch Frances and Lisbeth Ann told him they were going to get ready to go out. It was half-past three when he next saw them, in which time he had ransacked the book-shelves and settled himself down with a novel.

He had read and skipped nearly a half of it when Lisbeth Ann appeared.

"Good gracious, Johnny, aren't you ready yet?"

"I was ready an hour and a half ago except for putting on my coat. What the dickens can you women find to do in so much time?"

"That, my lad, is something you'll find out in due course," said Frances from the doorway. "Let's get moving."

She brought the car round to the front gate, and ordered Crompton into the back. Lisbeth Ann joined her in the front seat, and for an hour they ran through the riverside villages as far as Danesby, and there Frances began to double back on her course. It was shortly after half-past four that she pulled in at the Ferryman Inn, near Thorpe Bridge.

"I remembered that she does teas," Frances said laconically. "I suppose she has to do so to make the place pay. It must have a deadly trade for the duration of the winter months."

It was obvious that she had visited the inn on previous occasions, for she pushed open the front door and led the way to the dining room. She chose a table by the window, and as soon as all were seated the landlady arrived.

She paused in the doorway for a moment, started slightly, and then said: "Good afternoon, Mrs. Mundeham."

Frances gave her a friendly smile as she returned the greeting. "You can give us tea?"

"I serve anybody," she answered frostily. "Cartwright taught me that was the secret of good hostelry."

"I'm sure he was right, Mrs. Cartwright," Frances said sweetly.

Crompton looked her over. She was short, black-haired, and bright-eyed. She wore too-long pendant ear-rings, and wore too much eye-shadow and lipstick. Glancing at her bust, Crompton decided that she had just that bit too much of everything. Otherwise she would have been a comely bint.

"And what would you like?" Mrs. Cartwright asked shortly.

Frances glanced at Lisbeth Ann and Crompton. "Ham salads? Yes, three ham salads, please, with cakes to follow—"

"Tea for three, and bread-and-butter," nodded Mrs. Cartwright.

Frances chatted brightly about nothing in particular throughout the meal, and when the landlady brought in the cakes she said: "By the way, Mrs. Cartwright, we shall probably be calling in later this evening for a drink, so if Harry Davidson should call will you please tell him I'd like to see him?"

Crompton afterwards said that the silence that followed was one of the longest he could remember.

At last Mrs. Cartwright said: "Why should you think that Harry Davidson will come here?"

Frances smiled at her. "But he will come, won't he, Mrs. Cartwright?"

And then she added: "Or is he here already, Jenny? I may call you that? You're a younger woman than I am, and an attractive young woman. . . ."

Mrs. Cartwright sat on the edge of a nearby chair, and spread her hands on her thighs. "What are you getting at, Mrs. Mundeham?"

"I'm sorry if I've given you the impression that I'm after anything," replied Frances. "I would just like a word with Harry Davidson, quite privately, if and when he comes here. As for why he should come here at all, well, he is interested in you, isn't he? There's every reason why he should be so, too."

Mrs. Cartwright leaned forward. "Do you know where he is?"

Frances shook her head. "No, I do not—truthfully."

A frown appeared on the young widow's forehead. "Neither do I, and that's what's bothering me. . . ."

She paused for a few minutes, a few long minutes during which no one spoke, and then she stretched a hand and grasped Frances's arm. "Look, we've never liked each other—"

"We've never been enemies," Frances interrupted. "Is there anything I can do?"

"You'd—you'd really help me, Mrs. Mundeham!"

"I'd really help you for the simple reason that if I helped you I'd probably be helping someone else at the same time. What is it you wish me to do?"

Mrs. Cartwright looked hard at Crompton. "First, who's he?"

"Sorry I didn't introduce him. This is John Crompton, the *Borough News* reporter who is suspected by the police of killing Edward Packman. You can trust him."

"Harry didn't like you," Mrs. Cartwright said bluntly. "What are you doing here with Mrs. Mundeham? You don't look the sort to murder an old man!"

"I didn't," said Crompton, "and I've nothing against Harry Davidson. Not much, that is!"

"You're a reporter," she stated flatly. "Harry always says they're as good as the police. You can help Mrs. Mundeham. I want to find Harry. Somebody's got him somewhere, or he'd have come straight here. I could have hidden him so's nobody would find him—he knows that. Look, the police haven't got him, have they?"

Crompton shook his head. "I should have known. In any case, the police can't do such things. They have to bring a man before a magistrate and charge him if they have anything against him."

"There's somebody evil about," said Mrs. Cartwright. "I tell you Harry could have been safe here—and I still don't think he's done anything wrong!"

Frances, suave as ever, calmly poured three more cups of tea. "Care to have a cup with us, Jenny?" she asked.

Mrs. Cartwright rose and backed to the door. "No, thanks, ma'am. Never take food or drink with a customer, Cartwright used to say. It isn't right. And you needn't bother about the bill, ma'am."

"Oh, but we must," said Frances. "I'm sure Mr. Cartwright would agree with me. It is bad manners to accept free food from those whose living depends on it—or so Mundeham used to tell me. Husbands are very wise, Jenny. Perhaps you and I are in the best position to know, for we've both lost ours."

"Well, as you say, ma'am. I'll bring the check presently."

As the young widow left them, Frances gave Crompton a real eye-slammer of a wink, and in a loud voice suggested that he leave the meringue for her as she was very fond of them, and especially when they were home-made.

"You two-faced little cat," Crompton said in little more than a whisper.

"You should learn to be a tom," Frances said with a chuckle. "I'll bet Harry is!"

Later, Frances gave the signal to leave. "We'll put something on the table for her. I don't think she wants to see us again."

Crompton took a pound note from his wallet and laid it under the edge of his plate. Then they went back to the car and began the run home in the dusk to Rainley.

"Suppose you were in Davidson's position, and needed a hideout, where would you go?" Frances asked over her shoulder.

"If I really was Davidson, I should without doubt make for the Ferryman."

"And the widow!"

"Oh, Johnny!" protested Lisbeth Ann. "She's just an over-painted—"

"Shush, child!" said Frances. "She's over-painted, I'll agree, but she's also a very young widow who is very, very lonely. I'm not awfully keen on her, but I do hope Davidson is good to her! You know, Johnny, I really thought Harry Davidson would be there."

"And that's why you came out?"

"Oh yes. I wanted to ask him something."

"Wanted to ask him what—?"

"A question."

"Here we go again," complained Crompton. "The boy isn't fit to listen to secrets. Wait until he's in bed, and then we won't have to spell out what we have to say."

"As a matter of fact," said Frances, "I was going to do a spot of detective work for Mr. Crossley. He seems to believe that Davidson overheard an important conversation, and the only reason they were bringing him back from Manchester was to question him in the hope of proving that one way or the other. Reg says—"

"Who says?" interrupted Crompton.

"Er—Mr. Crossley says he thinks Davidson believes he is trying to pin Edward's death on him, and that is why he ran away. The next question is, if he isn't at the Ferryman, where on earth is he?"

Crompton shrugged in the darkness of the car. "It's easy enough to dodge. Just keep on the move, having bed and breakfast at an hotel or boarding house in one town, and then get cracking somewhere else for the next night, and so on. He could keep on the run for months that way—if the money held out. Anyway, how did you know about Davidson being keen on Jenny Cartwright?"

"You knew that Edward and I visited these riverside inns? Well, Edward out of the office, with a few shorts inside him, was a jovial character who liked to chaff people like Jenny. Davidson was often up there, and the idiot actually became jealous of Edward—as if Edward would undertake anything serious while I was with him! Davidson gave himself away, and the locals did quite a lot of winking and nodding to each other over Harry. He used to lean on the bar counter, following every movement she made."

"With a figure like that there are plenty she can make," said Crompton.

"Don't be coarse," said Lisbeth Ann, half-turning.

"It's my gift for the neat phrase coming out," said Crompton. "Didn't you know I'm going to be a writer!"

"We're home," said Frances. She turned the car into the drive and stopped the engine.

They had been in the house no more than quarter of an hour, and were enjoying a drink of light sherry, when the telephone rang. Frances went to the hall, and came back to tell Crompton it was some unknown caller asking for him.

He went through and picked up the handset. "Crompton here!"

"Is there anyone with you?" asked a familiar voice on the line. "I don't want anyone at that end to know who's calling. Get that?"

"Ye-es," said Crompton, "but who is it?"

"It's Charlie Carrington. I know where Davidson is, and I want you with me while we question him—and before Bowden and company get hold of him. Come straight to town."

"Can't," Crompton said shortly. "I'm not supposed to leave the two women. I'm staying all night."

"But he's here in town, and he can't get out! Isn't Mrs. M. armed in some way or other?"

"I believe she's got a small revolver."

"Nice and handy in case she should need it?"

Crompton lowered his voice. "Judging by conversation I overheard she keeps it in her dressing-table drawer."

"In that case," said Carrington, "you've nothing to worry about. They can lock the doors, and will be all right until you get back. You shouldn't be away from them for more than an hour or so."

"Okay," said Crompton. "I'll be with you—but where?"

"I'll wait for you outside the office, and I can do the rest of the journey on your pillion. Cheers for now." Crompton went back to break the news that he was leaving them for an hour.

"And where would you be going?" asked Frances.

Crompton sniffed. "You wouldn't understand, being a woman," he said in a tone of mock superiority. "This is my turn to have a secret!"

He pulled on his coat and helmet and went round to the garage for his scooter. He sped along the country roads at a good pace, and when only half a mile from the outskirts of Carrbank he had to slacken his pace as a car blazed towards him, its headlights blinding.

Then it stopped, and Crossley suddenly appeared before him.

"Where the hell do you think you're going!" he demanded. "I asked you to stay with the girls!"

"I've had a message—to get to Carrbank as soon as I could."

"Who phoned you?"

"Charlie Carrington. He rang up—well, from the office, I think."

Crossley gave vent to an oath, an expression of disgust. "You'd fall for anything! Anyway, tuck in behind us, and ignore the speed limit. The sooner we get to Rainley the less chance there is of Frances and Lisbeth Ann getting their throats cut! There's bloody murder waiting outside that cottage right now!"

Then he was inside the car, and it leapt away into the darkness. Crompton swung round in the narrow roadway and followed them. For some inner reason which he could not divine it had suddenly become all-important for him to reach Lisbeth Ann—before she got her throat cut.

"I'll murder Davidson!" he exclaimed as he rammed into top gear and chased the police car.

14
EVEN MY OWN GRANNY

THE POLICE CAR braked so suddenly outside the cottage that Crompton nearly rammed it. Crossley jumped out and ran down the garden path, and the C.I.D. sergeant driving took up a position at the gate. As Crompton leaned the scooter against the white paling there came a roar from Crossley inside the cottage, and from somewhere at the rear came a scream from Lisbeth Ann. Then, in the light of the stars, Crompton saw her running along the lane, chased by a man who was gaining on her.

Crompton started the scooter, flung himself into the saddle, and roared off in pursuit. He was hoping to cut off the pursuer where the lane, passing behind the three neighbouring cottages, joined the main road, but he was too late, and both Lisbeth Ann and the man disappeared into the shadows of the copse that hugged the edge of the towpath.

Lisbeth Ann screamed again, and choked. Crompton switched on his headlight, and opened the throttle, making the scooter buck and jump on the uneven footpath.

Fifty yards ahead, Lisbeth Ann was rolling and kicking in the grass, fighting off the man who was trying to strangle her. Then her assailant suddenly threw her back as the headlight struck him, and began to run down the path to the river.

Crompton drove straight past Lisbeth Ann. Twenty yards further on, as he came almost alongside the running figure, he closed his throttle, slipped into neutral, and then flung himself sideways. "This is it, Davidson!" he exclaimed.

The man broke free, and slammed him hard over the right arm with the end of a broken tree branch. Then he laughed, and Crompton stared through the darkness.

"Charlie Carrington!"

"Charlie Carrington—and you'll never take me! But you can take that, and that, and that . . . !"

Blows rained on Crompton's head, and although he tried to close with Carrington his senses were slipping away from him, and he sank down to his knees.

Carrington gave him another blow for good measure, and then lifted the scooter, swung himself into the saddle, and started the engine. He put it into gear and rode off down the path.

Crompton rolled over and tried to rise, and then Lisbeth Ann was on her knees beside him, lifting his head and sobbing. "Johnny! Johnny! Are you all right, darling? Johnny!"

Crompton tried hard to think, and then he put his arms round her and drew her down to him. "My God, Lisbeth Ann, I love you! I think I've loved you for a long time."

"I know you have," she sobbed, "and it's been such a long time waiting for you to wake up."

Running footsteps disturbed them, heavy and desperate footsteps, and then Crossley was calling anxiously. "Lisbeth Ann! Crompton! Where are you?"

"We're here," answered Lisbeth Ann, and then Crossley nearly fell over them.

"What a hell of a time to make love in a wood!" he exclaimed.

"Carrington laid me out with half a tree," Crompton said feebly. "He's ridden off down the path on my scooter."

"I can hear it," said Crossley. "He's driving straight to the river. Listen. . . ."

In the night stillness they could hear both the engine, and the bump of the tyres as Carrington sped down the rough path. There came a high-pitched scream, a heavy splash, and a throaty cry for help.

Crossley chased down the path to the river, and Crompton, his head throbbing painfully, followed more slowly with Lisbeth Ann. When they eventually came up to Crossley he was standing on the high bank, his hands on his hips.

"He's gone," he said shortly. "Looking for him on a night like this is like looking for a black cat in a coal cellar."

"I'll go in if you like," said Crompton, and began stripping off his coat.

Crossley touched his arm in the half-darkness. "No, perhaps it's better this way, Johnny. He'll probably be a quarter of a mile down-river by this time—it's a fast current down to the weir. We'll get your bike out in daylight."

"Oh, damn the bike," said Crompton. Then, urgently, he asked: "What about Frances?"

"She's safe, but shocked. You know what happened? No, of course you don't! Carrington rang up from the village telephone box, and as soon as you'd set off for town he went to the cottage and knocked at the door. As Frances answered it he knocked her out cold, and went straight upstairs and came down with her revolver. . . ."

"And I told him where it was!" Crompton said bitterly.

"Lisbeth Ann can tell you the rest."

"I heard Frances go down, and heard someone come downstairs. Then, as I got to the hall, Charlie came from the dining-room doorway with the revolver. He said Frances was carrying a document he wanted. I was to strip her and find it. He said he'd searched the house, and everywhere else where it was likely to be, and it must be somewhere on her person.

"I tried hard to think, and I said we had to get her into the lounge where it was warm if I was going to undress her.

He told me to stand back, and then with one hand dragged her through to the hearth. He was bending as he dragged her through, so I got the poker and hit him across the wrist so that he dropped the revolver. He called me a damned bitch, and came for me. I dodged round the furniture, and out into the hall.

"He had just about got me cornered when I saw the kitchen door was open, so I ran through and flung the door back in his face. Then I went out by the back way, down the back-garden path, and out to the lane. I knew my way through the copse, and I thought I could perhaps lose him there. Then he caught up with me and tripped me. You know the rest."

"And what about Davidson?" asked Crompton.

"Bowden's attending to him. The fool went straight to Carrington for help when he dodged our man at Sheffield. Carrington fed him whisky until he was nearly squiffed, and then he and Cora carried him upstairs to the attic and tied him down to the bed. I rather suspected he was in the house when you and I called. You see, Johnny, it was Carrington who did the two breakings and enterings at Frances's cottage, searched Packman's office and home, and then did a phoney at his home to throw us off the scent, but it wasn't a good enough job to fool me. I let him think I was satisfied, and then put the house under observation. Lights appearing in the attic at what should be meal-times supplied the rest of the answers."

He shivered. "Nippy, isn't it? Let's get back to the cottage, and then the best man on his feet can do something about a warm drink. I hope it will be Frances. She makes darned good coffee."

"Got friendly with her, haven't you?" asked Crompton softly.

"We-ell, I'm a bachelor, Johnny," Crossley replied. "You'll agree it isn't much of a life for a man, and she's a lovely little lady, and—oh blast it, why fence! I'm in love with her!"

Lisbeth Ann squeezed his arm. "Good luck—Uncle Reginald!"

"So Charlie killed Packman," murmured Crompton. "How the deuce did he manage it?"

"Charlie Carrington was no man's fool—in the main. He knew, somehow, that he'd shot his bolt with Packman when he refused to write up the Danny Moss story as Packman wanted it. So had you as a reporter! Davidson was present, or somewhere near, when Packman told Carrington he was making a new will on the grounds that Charlie wasn't good enough to have a share in running the paper after his death."

"If you haven't seen Davidson, how do you know?"

"Davidson hiccupped the story out to young Seymour the night before the murder, and Seymour says that Davidson told him that Charlie told him he'd never live to make a new will. That's hearsay, and not evidence, but Davidson will probably come clean after a long interview at the warehouse. We can't do anything to him as regards the pillory part of the business, because Packman was then dead, but for just so long as Davidson doesn't realise that he's likely to be co-operative."

"Yes," said Crompton, "but you still haven't told me when Charlie did it!"

"I told you Charlie was no man's fool," said Crossley as they left the copse and came to the main road. "He knew the movements of everyone concerned. You went out by the Market Place exit, and he dodged out—ostensibly to the toilets—to the Gate. He'd a full minute and a half advantage.

"The rest I can only surmise. With all the men at break he could get at Packman all right, and if you came in and found Packman dead or dying you weren't likely to start searching the premises, were you?"

"No-o," said Crompton. "Considering the previous row I should probably have acted on my first impulse and got out like a hare—although I think I should have come clean with you when I'd got myself straightened."

"Which you did after finding him," said Crossley. "Still, Charlie was lucky, and found him downstairs. If, as you said, Packman was busy checking the page proof, he wouldn't be likely to turn round when Charlie spoke to him, so that was that. One good blow, and out like lightning. He probably hid in the works until you went in, and then dodged out again while you were standing flabbergasted at finding Packman dead. The fact that you went into the Bells for a steadier was also in his favour, and he was back in position at the Falcon when you returned. I had natters with Morgan and Newnes, and they couldn't say whether Carrington was in or out. You reporters apparently circulate from room to room in search of possible contacts and stories, and they weren't even aware that Charlie had left them for a few minutes. No, he had all the breaks in addition to a good brain turned to wrongful uses!"

"And Seymour went on guard just after Charlie was clear."

"Oh well," said Crossley, "here we are."

They found Frances sitting by the fire, and the sergeant keeping her company. She smiled wanly, and fingered her chin. "This is something even my husband never did to me."

"You all right?" Crossley asked anxiously.

"I will be," she said. "And Carrington?"

"Drove straight into the river on Johnny's bike," Crossley said shortly. "He first tried to strangle Lisbeth Ann, then laid Johnny out with a tree, and then drove into the river. No trace."

"It's been quite an evening. I think I'll get us all a drink of coffee," said Frances, rising.

Crossley took her arm solicitously. "Sure you're all right? Look, I'll come and help you."

She gave him a grateful smile. The sergeant looked at Lisbeth Ann and Crompton, and coughed. "Think I ought to see if the car's all right. Give me a call when the coffee's ready, won't you?"

When he had gone they stood quietly for a minute, and from the kitchen they heard Crossley telling Frances that it was a very remote place for a woman to live in alone, and that she really wanted a man to look after her.

"Perhaps I do," she answered softly. "I shall have to think about looking for one."

Then the kitchen door was closed gently.

"Johnny . . ." said Lisbeth Ann.

"Eh?" he asked, rousing himself from a reverie.

"Can you remember what you said to me in the copse?"

"Er—yes. Why?"

Lisbeth Ann bent to pick up the heavy poker from the hearth. "This is harder than the branch Charlie hit you with. Do I have to use it, or could you—please—say it again?"

She moved closer to him. Crompton just stared into her eyes for a few moments, and then put his arms round her and kissed her.

They were standing there five minutes later when Crossley opened the door for Frances to carry in the tray.

"Sorry I've been a long time, darlings, but the milk boiled over—"

She paused and smiled. "Don't mind us! We're grown up."

"Johnny's going to marry me!" Lisbeth Ann said happily.

"He stands need to if that's the way he makes love," said Frances. "I may have news for you two later—about Reg and myself. Later, that is. There are some things persons can do, and some they can't do without offending public opinion. Now where is our sergeant?"

Crompton fetched him in, and then Frances, having served the coffee, excused herself for a few moments. She came back with a flushed smile. "I've had it hidden for days between me and my—er—corsets. It's Edward's will. I don't know what's in it, but it was witnessed by the Vicar of St. Saviour's Church, and both churchwardens just for make-weight. I'll open it . . ."

She glanced at Crossley. "Shall I read it?"

He nodded.

"It begins in the usual way about last will and testament, and continues: It was my original intention, considering that my niece, Lisbeth Ann, holds a half-share in the *Borough News*, to balance her inexperience by willing my share equally to Mrs. Frances Mundeham, my dear friend, and to Charles Carrington. Mrs. Mundeham, like Lisbeth Ann, knows nothing of newspapers, and recent events have satisfied me that Charles Carrington is not a suitable person to have any measure of control in the *Borough News*. A newspaper should be controlled, managed, and edited by newspapermen, and the introduction of amateurs can do no more than damage the name of the paper. At one time I had considered the substitution of John Crompton, my present chief reporter, for Charles Carrington, but there again recent events convince me that while he is an excellent journalist and reporter he is totally unsuited to undertake the management of my paper. It is my wish, therefore, that my share of the *Borough News* should be offered to the proprietors of the Burnham newspaper group, and the proceeds of such sale shall go to the said Mrs. Frances Mundeham in their entirety. It is my further wish that my niece, Lisbeth Ann Grosvenor, shall retain her holding in the *Borough News* so that some small part of the paper which was built up by my father and myself shall remain in the family."

"Carrington would certainly have been wild if he'd heard that read out!" commented Crompton.

"I rather fancy that Packman had told him in even more violent words," said Crossley.

"So tomorrow we start making up for lost time and begin to get the paper out once more—and for how long?" said Crompton.

"Have you any money saved up, Johnny?" Frances asked unexpectedly.

"Yes, but why on earth . . . ?"

"The cottage next door but one is coming empty in three months. We could arrange for you to rent it, and you could write in your spare time."

"Well, if you know the landlord . . . I'm sick of digs, and I have the scooter. . . ."

"You've also asked me to marry you," Lisbeth Ann said firmly.

Crompton blinked. "Oh, you mean for us to get married in three months, and live here in Rainley?"

Frances nodded vigorously. "The cottage is mine. I own the whole row."

She frowned. "Johnny Crompton! What *are* you thinking about? I'm talking to you!"

"Sorry," said Crompton. "I was just thinking. Packman warned him when he first went to see him, and I think it will be poetic justice."

"What will, you peculiar man?"

Crompton stared at her dreamily, and waved a hand across the room. "Forty-eight-point Century across the whole page—*Death Drive After Murder*, or *Local Author*—"

"Johnny!" Lisbeth Ann almost shouted.

"Eh? What?"

"A four-column picture as we're coming out of church, with Frances as matron of honour, Reg as best man, and—"

Crossley tapped Frances on the arm. "They should make a go of it. They're both affected with the same madness."

The sergeant grinned, and passed his cup for a refill.

"Even your own granny," said Frances, and smiled affectionately at Crompton and Lisbeth Ann.

THE END